AMISH STAR

This Little Amish Light Series - Book 1

RACHEL STOLTZFUS

CONTENTS

GET THE RACHEL STOLTZFUS
STARTER LIBRARY FOR FREE.

Get the Rachel Stoltzfus Starter Library for FREE.

Sign up to receive new release updates and discount books from Rachel Stoltzfus, and you'll get Rachel's 5-Book Starter library, including Book 1 of Amish Country Tours, and four more great Amish books.

Details can be found at the end of this book.

ISBN-13:978-1721985517
ISBN-10:1721985514

She has the voice of an angel. Will she plummet or soar?

Sixteen-year-old Gracie Troyer's beautiful voice is a gift from Gott. When a pair of Englisch talent scouts hear her singing at a local market, they are delighted with the possibility of introducing her to the wider world. Gracie doesn't want to defy her Ordnung, but she begins to wonder if it's truly right to "hide her light under a bushel." Gott has given her a gift. Maybe she can share Gott's light and love with the world...and she is on her rumspringe, so it can't be all bad.

But as Gracie struggles to find her place in the competitive world of Englisch music, her relationship with her community, and a young, fragile growing love, will both be threatened. Can Gracie let her light shine without losing everything else she loves?

Find out in Amish Star, Book 1, the first book of the This Little Amish Light series. Amish Star is an uplifting, Christian romance about the power of faith and the gifts we all share.

CHAPTER 1

Gracie grinned. The day had been gut for her—almost all of her baked goods had sold, meaning she could give a considerable amount of money to her mamm. As she smiled, the dimple in her right cheek winked. Gathering her containers, she began to nest them inside each other for washing later on. As she did so, she lapsed into one of her favorite hymns from the Ausbund.

Those who knew of Gracie's voice, and her habit of singing when happy, smiled. Strangers and the Englisch who were new to Crawford County stopped to listen to the clear, sweet voice rising out around them. Two people, Paul and Melody Wilson, closed their eyes and even though they couldn't recognize the German words, marked the time with their fingers tapping the air. When Gracie finished singing, the last pure note evaporated in the air, just like the cleanest, iciest snowflake. Looking at his wife, Paul allowed his chin to drop. "Mel, we gotta get her! For the show!"

"Let's see if she knows something that's a pretty common hymn. C'mon! Melody responded, excited to hear more. Approaching the Troyer booth, Melody smiled at Gracie, sticking her hand out. "Hi, my name is Melody Wilson and this is my husband, Paul. We heard your beautiful voice! If you would, do you know 'Amazing Grace?'"

Gracie, taken by surprise, looked awkwardly at her mamm, Abigail Troyer. "Mamm, should I?"

Abigail, thinking the couple wanted to worship Gott, nodded. "Sing for them." She didn't stop her quick, practiced movements, putting the empty bakery containers away.

"Uh…okay." Gracie shrugged slightly, feeling embarrassed. This was the first time any Englisch had ever approached her about singing. Looking nervously at the beautiful Englisch woman and her husband, Gracie licked her lips and swallowed, wishing she hadn't finished all her water earlier. Expanding her diaphragm and filling her lungs with air, she started. "A-mazing gra-a-ace, how swe-e-et the sound…" As she sang, she clasped the fingers of one hand in the other, closed her eyes and allowed the song's words and rhythm to take her away. When the last note faded away, Gracie's eyes slowly opened and she returned to the warm, noisy Amish store.

"Oh…my…Goodness! Paul, she has the voice of an angel! Sweetie, we need to get you into a talent competition!"

Hearing the word "competition," Gracie immediately panicked. "Nee! I can't!" Grabbing her baking containers into her arms, and not caring that she was dropping several, she immediately turned and ran toward the exit, her mother close behind. "I would be breaking our Ordnung!" Once in the buggy, she turned, wide-eyed toward Abigail. "Mamm, how did that happen? Nobody has ever done that before!"

Abigail's hands on the reins were trembling and she prayed the more sensitive of their horses wouldn't pick up on that tiny motion and refuse to go home. Fortunately, Girlie moved quickly toward home, looking forward to grain, water and her stall.

Gracie, feeling tension curling and gathering in her back, shoulders and stomach, turned around, praying she wouldn't see the Englisch couple behind them.

"Are those people there?"

"Nee, thank Gott. It's just us and a few of our neighbors." Breathing out on purpose, Gracie's eyes closed and she allowed the tension to leave her body. "I don't like what happened there."

"Me either."

⚜

Back in the Amish store, the Englisch couple looked around warily, suddenly aware that they stuck out as the "foreigners" they were. Paul swallowed, gave a lame smile and asked, "So…what did we do there? We thought we were complimenting her, because her voice is…well, not to overstate it, but heavenly."

The community's deacon, Eli Bontrager, stepped forward. He had no answering smile and his arms were crossed tightly over his chest. "Ya, she does. It's a gift from Gott and that's just how we regard her voice. Perhaps you don't know much about our practices here. But we frown on competition, on consciously directing attention to oneself. Because we try not to stand out, to make ourselves 'seem better' than others. When Miss Troyer sings, she does so simply to give glory to Gott. If you've made your purchases, maybe you should leave. You're making the others nervous."

Melody wanted to make their position clear. "We'll leave, but first, we're new here. We just moved to Philadelphia from out of state. And yes...we..." she gulped, realizing almost too late that she shouldn't mention that they were talent promoters for a beloved television talent competition, *The Country's Most Talented*. "We loved her voice. We just didn't know. Please, extend our sincerest apologies to Miss...Troyer, was it?"

Eli hid a grimace. He would have been better saying Gracie's first name. Now, they could try to find her using her last name. "Ya. Please leave. We'll pass your message along."

Quickly, the Wilsons took off, clutching their purchases close to their bodies, as though fearing they'd be pulled away from them. It wasn't until they got to their late-model Subaru that Paul finally let out a deep, noisy breath. "Man, talk about stepping right in it!"

Melody dropped down into the passenger seat and dropped her head back. She groaned loudly. "My Goodness, you'd think we said something completely embarrassing to her! We complimented the girl!"

As she spoke, Abe Lapp, Gracie's boyfriend, was walking by. He heard what Melody said. Leaning down, he rested his forearms on the driver's window and peered in. His usual friendly smile was absent. "Excuse me. Ya, you gave her a compliment. Two things. First, we don't usually compliment others for something that Gott has given to them. We don't want them to become full of pride. Second, I suggest you go to the library or use that internet to do some research on us. It's out there."

Paul was incurably optimistic and daring. Even knowing that Abe was so upset, he stuck one finger into the air and spoke. "Good idea. Once we do, we'd like to approach this girl and speak to her in more detail. We feel she should—"

"Should...what?" Abe's voice was deceptively quiet. All expression was wiped from his face.

Paul, seeing this shrugged. "Um...she should know just what it is she's turning down."

"Let me explain just a little more. She doesn't have to know any more. We have seen Englisch television when we go to the restaurant in town. We are aware that there are many of these 'talent contests' that pit hopeful people against each other. If they want to do that, it's fine. We aren't going to judge them. But we want to be left alone to live our own lives and follow our beliefs. Do you understand?" Here, Abe stood straight and took a few steps from the car. It was a clear invitation that the interlopers should leave.

Paul took the hint. Starting the engine, he nodded

once and, looking around, put the car into gear and drove away. As he drove, he was quiet, just thinking.

Melody spoke. "What he said, Paul, about not judging or stopping people who aren't Amish from our competition? That's unusual."

"Yeah, I agree. It is. His suggestion's good, actually. Let's pick up a few books on the Amish and see what we can find online. Maybe it'll help us to approach this Miss Troyer in a way that won't freak her out." Paul reached the expressway heading back to Philadelphia, wanting to be home right away. "I really want to get her into the show." From then on, he lapsed into silence.

✺

At home, Gracie calmed down as she washed all of her bakery containers. As she did so, she sang a hymn, and then stopped abruptly. "Mamm?"

"Ya, what is it, Gracie?"

"If I hadn't been singing, that wouldn't have happened. Maybe I shouldn't sing in public anymore." Gracie's face was set in an uncharacteristic pout.

"Nee, daughter! You were praising Gott in the

best way you knew! Keep singing and don't let people like them stop you."

Jon Troyer, Gracie's daed, came into the kitchen from outside. "What happened? Gracie, why do you look so unhappy?"

Gracie sighed, indicating quietly to Abigail that she could tell the whole sorry story.

"Husband, we were counting our money, selling the last of our goods and getting ready to load up and come home. Gracie began singing one of her favorite hymns. An Englisch couple walked up. We've never seen them at the market before today, so they are new. As soon as Gracie finished singing, they went up to her and said that they wanted to sign her up for some competition that takes place on television! Grace told them no and ran."

"My Gott. I'm glad she responded that way. Gracie, don't worry so much. You did everything just as you should have." Jon looked at Abigail, his next words directed at her. If you see those foreigners anywhere around, looking for Gracie, you get her away from them. I'll do the same."

"Ya. I think…nee, I pray…that, because we've never seen them around here, they are just new to our culture and beliefs." Still, Abigail sighed. "Sometimes, I wish we could just approach and educate them! Now, we have to worry about them stalking our daughter, just because of a gift she was given from Gott." Today, more than ever, Abigail felt the yawning divide between her faith and Englischer's.

"I'm just not going to sing in public anymore. Ever." Gracie was still highly upset.

"Nee, daughter, we all benefit from the blessing of your voice." Jon forced himself to relax as he looked at Gracie. Along with her beautiful voice, she had also been born extremely sensitive. She would know if he was upset just by looking at him. "Look at me, daughter." As her eyes focused on him, he continued. "Please, don't ever deny yourself the opportunity to praise Gott with song. Ya, we benefit from hearing you. What I would suggest is that in the future you make sure everyone in the area has heard you singing before, ya?"

Gracie thought for several seconds, and then sighed. Her shoulders and back relaxed. "Okay, ya. I will."

"Gut. Now, make yourself some tea and shake this off."

A t home, Abe Lapp paced back and forth in the carpentry shop his daed owned. He kept clenching his fists as he tried to calm down.

"Son, what is wrong with you? You look like you're ready to explode!"

Abe explained what had happened to Gracie earlier at the market. "I am furious! After, I overhead them in their car, talking about how they'd complimented her voice. Then the woman's husband said they wanted her to know what she's giving up. Daed, I am not a violent man, but I was really tempted in that moment...so I told them that they should do their research about our beliefs and our culture. I dared say nothing more, or I would be facing the elders right now."

"Son, you did everything you could to protect her." Ben suspected that Abe had been seeing Gracie for some time, but due to the traditional secrecy around Amish dating practices, he didn't know for sure. "Just protect her. As you would any of your friends. And be on the lookout for these people to come back. Something tells me they won't stop."

Abe began pacing again, feeling the anger as tension in his neck and shoulders. "I agree. They won't stop." From that day on, Abe was on the lookout for the Wilsons. While he didn't know their names, he remembered what they looked like and what they drove. Every time he went outside, he felt fine threads of tension running through his body as he looked for signs of the couple. Even when he didn't spot them, he was aware they could pop up at any time.

O n Friday night, Gracie and Abe met their friends at the diner just outside their community. Everyone was aware of what had happened to Gracie. Either they kept an eye on her out of curiosity or they allowed their eyes to scan the area, looking for the couple that had approached her the day before.

Gracie still felt a little uneasy. Even inside the diner, she kept her cloak on over her shoulders, as if it would protect her from any unwanted approaches. She sat back in the booth, next to Abe and her closest friend, Miriam King.

"Gracie, why are you trying to hide? They aren't here. And even if they do show up, you have all of us to keep them from getting to you."

Gracie, feeling nervous, allowed her eyes to roam

around the area. "Denki, Miriam. I just feel so stupid. There I was, singing and they heard me!"

"What did your daed say?" Miriam had spent some time living with the Troyers, when her daed was very ill several years earlier.

"To keep singing. And just to be watchful, in case they come back."

"Okay. Gut. There's being watchful, and then there's allowing your eyes to leave your head, like they are on little buggy stalks, just waving all around." Miriam's face contorted as she opened her eyes as wide as they could go. She waggled her fingers next to her face.

Gracie had to giggle. Miriam had always been able to pull her out of her bad, worrying moods. She felt the nerves and tension leaving her back and neck. "Okay, I'm hungry. What are we going to eat?"

Abe nodded, smiling at Gracie. "Ya. I want to get to where we're going to hang out so we can have fun!" He didn't say that he felt they were too much in the open here—or that they were in the Wilson's territory. As much as he tried to hide it, he felt the tension and worry holding his lean muscles in a tightened bunch. Looking through the menu, he decided what he wanted to order. Giving the menu to Gracie, he urged her to order.

"Hmmm. I think I'll have the hot roast beef sandwich and veggies. Along with a hot coffee! It's going to be cold tonight!" Gracie looked at Abe. "What are you having?"

"That sandwich sounds like a wunderbaar idea."

Forty-five minutes later, after paying for their orders and leaving tips, the group of Amish youth departed the diner. Instead of coming in their buggies, they had all piled into two older, used vehicles, which two of the boys had bought.

"You know, Stephen, now that Gracie was singled out by Englischers, I'm glad we're in cars. It makes it harder for them to spot us."

"True, Abe. You know what would help more? Girls, remove your prayer caps, just until we get to the lookout. Abe, tell Joe to have the girls in his car do the same."

Abe was grateful for his best friend's suggestion. He immediately yelled it out to Joe, who passed the message on to the female passengers in his car.

Every girl quickly took off their prayer caps as the boys removed their hats. At the lookout point, everyone decided to keep their hats or coverings off, just in case. Gracie spoke up. "Even with no caps on, we're wearing our Plain clothing. We still stick out. Shouldn't we go to someone's barn or something?"

Everyone talked among themselves. Joe and

Stephen made the decision that they would relocate to Stephen's daed's barn.

In the barn, everyone relaxed, feeling as though they were safer in their own community. Gracie felt the nervous feeling leaving her body as she relaxed next to Abe. She accepted a can of pop as Abe opened a can of beer. They listened to rock music, laughing and talking. Some of the couples split off from the main group, seeking privacy for the activities they wanted to take part in. It was late when everyone finally piled into the cars to go home. Gracie still felt as though she had a target on her back. She scooched down in the back seat, practically burying her head into Abe's shoulder.

"You don't want to be seen outside the car?"

"Nee. I feel like they're still out there, looking around for me." Gracie's voice was quiet and it held a strong note of fear.

Abe sighed, feeling frustration for his girlfriend. "My Gott, I wish they would have just expressed appreciation for your singing, and then left you alone!"

Gracie, feeling the muscles in Abe's shoulders

bunching up, sat up. "Nee, Abe! Don't worry! All I can do is try to keep from being noticed."

"Well, then, that makes my suggestion for our date tomorrow night easy. Why don't we go into the city with the others—in Englisch clothing?"

Gracie had never attempted to leave her Plain clothing at home. The idea was new and a little bit scary. Pulling a breath deep into her chest, she thought for several seconds. Then, she realized that if she looked like any other teen girl, it would be harder to recognize her. "Ya. Okay. But we can't use the Pennsylvania Deitch at all!"

"Ya. So we'd better remind ourselves of that. Miriam told Stephen she can get you jeans and a T-shirt in your size. Wear your sneakers like usual. And leave your hair down or put it into a plain ponytail."

"That sounds gut. Uhh, good." Gracie giggled as Abe kissed her deeply. In the house, she walked quietly upstairs, still smiling.

༺✦༻

The next night, Gracie quickly changed upstairs at Miriam's.

"Here, let me do your hair. I'm thinking just a braided ponytail, so you'll look like a high school girl."

"Ya, that sounds...um, yeah that sounds good. I need to make myself remember!"

Miriam, taking Gracie's long, straight auburn hair down, giggled." Me, too. We'll practice in the car. I know Stephen and Abe want to take us to an Applebee's in Philadelphia. And that sounds gut...good!" Untangling Gracie's hair, Miriam expertly put it into a ponytail, and then braided it. "'There. You look wonderful! Just like a high school girl."

"Do your parents know why we're dressing like this?"

"Yeah. I told them exactly what happened to you. Remember that I have the booth across from you! They support making it look like we're not Amish."

That admission stunned Gracie. Looking at Miriam with wide eyes, she expressed her shock. "I'd think they want us to stay in our Plain clothing as much as possible."

"Normally, ya...yeah. But they don't want to see you being bothered by that couple, so they told me that they much preferred that we dress as Englischers."

"Where are we meeting the boys?"

"Down the road. We'd better go so we don't get to Philadelphia too late." Miriam led the way downstairs. "Daed, Mamm, we're going now. We'll be back home before it gets too late."

"And where will you be tonight?"

"Applebee's in Philadelphia." Miriam adjusted her T-shirt so it was more comfortable. She carried a faded denim jacket in one hand, handing a second one to Gracie.

"Girls, please be careful there. If you see those people again, do everything you can to get away."

"Oh, Missus King, you don't have to tell me that twice! I will be so careful and I will get away from those people, too." Gracie felt goosebumps rising on her arms at the memory of what had happened to her the previous week.

Hurrying down the road, the girls slipped the jackets on, grateful for the additional warmth they gave. Even though the Englischer clothing was so foreign to them, they were glad to be wearing outfits that allowed them to blend in better. In Stephen's car, the two couples laughed and chatted all the way up to Philadelphia.

Gracie felt nervous as they got out of the car in the restaurant parking lot. She was happy to nestle into Abe's muscular side as they walked inside. She dipped her head down so nobody would recognize her face.

"Gracie? Why are you looking down? I don't see them here." Abe's quiet voice expressed concern for Gracie.

"Oh, thank Gott…God for that." Feeling more relaxed, Gracie looked up and all around them. Not seeing the Wilsons, she was finally able to relax all the way. Seated in a large booth with Abe and her closest friends, she read through the menu, trying to decide what to eat. As they ate their appetizers, they chatted about what they wanted to do in the city.

"I'd like to see that new movie. The Star Wars one." Stephen grinned.

Miriam shook her head slightly. "He is so obsessed with that movie series."

"I don't mind. I'd like to see it as well." Abe gave Stephen a high-five across the booth. "Gracie?"

Gracie looked at Miriam. She really wanted to go listen to some secular music. "What about going to an under-21 club? Listen to some rock?"

Abe nodded in approval. "That's a good one, too. Stephen?"

Stephen blew out a long breath. "Ach, Gracie! That's such a hard choice! Okay, let's do this. We'll come back here in a couple weeks and see the movie then. Deal?"

"Deal!" Meals arrived shortly after and Gracie dug into her chicken, enjoying the tart taste of the celery and apple topping. Both couples chatted and laughed at their jokes as they ate, looking forward to the rest of their evening.

I n the club, the boys ordered sodas for them and their girls. Gracie anticipated listening to the music and learning some new songs. Looking around, she saw other young people like them, boys and girls, who were out for a fun evening listening to music in the company of their friends. Looking at Miriam, she was grateful that they had worn regular clothing. She whipped her head around as the announcer spoke into the mic. "Miriam, they're starting!" Gracie leaned forward, wanting to be right on stage with the singers, learning their techniques.

Stephen and Abe listened to the music as well. But Abe found himself looking around the small venue, trying to see if he could spot either one of the Wilsons. His gaze rested on each face as he looked carefully. Not seeing either one, he relaxed, slipping his arm around Gracie's back. Still, he felt it necessary to check every so often. Close to the end of the second set, he saw Melody coming in, followed by her husband, Paul. "Hey, Steve! We gotta go. Now! They just came in!"

Gracie was reluctantly jolted out of the music-induced haze she'd been in. "What? Who?"

"Those people who want you for that contest.

Come on! Let's go!" Catching Gracie's hand in his, Abe didn't wait. Positioning Gracie between him and the wall, he shielded her from view. Looking quickly, he saw that Stephen and Miriam were right behind them. As they edged out, Abe prayed. *Gott, please get us out of here before they notice Gracie. Please, get us out of here!* He didn't breathe easily until they were outside. Still, he shielded Gracie with his tall, lean body.

Gracie was looking down again, crossing her arms tightly across her slender middle. She was angry. As they hurried to Stephen's car, she burst out. "Why did they ruin our night? I was learning so much, just listening to the singers!"

"I would have loved to stay as well. But I don't think your parents would have been happy if the Wilsons had been able to talk to you again."

"No, they wouldn't." Gracie slipped quickly into the car. She didn't dare to look around.

Abe looked back toward the club. Not seeing either one of the Wilsons following them, he let out a long sigh of relief. "Thank Gott. He kept them from following us."

"Ya. But you saw them. It was your fast action that protected me. That and Gott's help." Gracie slipped her hand into Abe's and squeezed.

Stephen navigated the streets, heading back

toward the expressway. He growled when he saw a long traffic backup ahead of them. "No way. I'm not waiting in that buncha' cars. I'll take a side road back home."

"Do you know the way?"

"Ya. Daed and I have taken it many times. It's like driving from home to the old bishop's house, it's that familiar." Soon, Stephen had guided the car onto the secondary highway. While the speed limit was lower than it would have been on the expressway, he knew that they would still be home at a reasonable hour. "Gracie? Do you think they were looking for you?"

Gracie thought for a few seconds. "Nee. I'm sure they know I won't sing secular music. It was just a lucky stop for them…well, not so lucky, since we got out before they knew I was there." Again, Gracie looked at Abe, giving him a tender, grateful smile.

"Well, I'm just glad Abe was looking around."

"Me, too. Abe, did you get a chance to enjoy the music?"

"Oh, ya. I did. But I didn't want them to surprise us, so I just looked around every few minutes. I really enjoyed their cover of Elvis Presley."

Gracie giggled. "Ya, you like that old music style."

Abe broke into a near-perfect rendition of "Hound Dog." Smiling at Gracie, he pulled a cellophane-wrapped CD out of his jacket. "I got this for you. I have one for me as well."

Gracie gasped. Looking at the cover, she saw that it was a Dolly Parton CD, featuring all gospel music. "Denki! It's perfect!"

"We'll listen to that away from both of our parents' houses. In the CD player I just bought last week." Abe's grin was happy. He was pleased that he'd found something Gracie would enjoy.

In the front seat, Stephen smiled at Miriam. "I have one for you as well. I'll give it to you before we get to your house."

Miriam grinned. The evening hadn't been ruined, after all.

The next evening, both couples were at the Sing. After playing a spirited game of baseball, everyone grabbed plates and loaded up with snacks and sodas. After the event ended, Abe drove Gracie home. "Ah, liebe, what a weekend. We had fun, didn't we?"

"Ya, we did." Gracie gasped, straightening out and looking carefully all around the buggy.

"What? What is it?"

"I…I feel like someone's staring at me!"

Abe looked all around them, wishing it wasn't already so dark. "Hold on." Bringing the reins down on his horses' backs, he chirruped at them. "Hurry!" In response, the horses sprang into a ground-eating canter. Soon, he turned as fast as he safely could onto a side road that led indirectly to the Troyer home. "Look behind us. Let me know if anyone's back there."

Gracie swept her gaze all around, from side to side. "Nee. No headlights. I don't hear a car, either."

Abe didn't slow down. He didn't trust the Wilsons as far as he could throw them. "Nearly to your house. I'm going to pull the team into the lean-to and go inside with you. I don't trust them not to sneak up and knock on the door."

"Okay." After they pulled into the yard, Abe stopped under the lean-to. She was grateful it wasn't too cold yet. They ran fast into the house, using the back door.

"Gracie! What is it?" Jon stood, letting several sheets of paper flutter to the floor unnoticed.

"We were on our way home from the sing and I felt like someone was just...staring at me. Abe got us here as fast as he could."

"Sir, I'm parked under the lean-to and I'd rather stay here until I know that whoever is out there won't bug Gracie. I think it's that couple that accosted her last week."

"I agree. Coffee?"

"Ya, denki." The couple waited for nearly half an hour before they decided that whoever had been spying on Gracie had long gone. "I think they realized you knew they were out there. And that it would be mupsich ot them to try and announce themselves here. Abe, I'm grateful for your actions getting her home."

"You're welcome. I'd better go. Daed and I have a busy day tomorrow. Lots of orders to work on."

"Ya. I need to make sure the crops are ready for harvesting tomorrow. I need to make sure my crew will be ready as well. Abe, you'd better go home and go to bed. Gracie, you have a busy day as well."

❧

Just outside the house and hidden by dense trees, Paul and Melody kept their gaze on the Troyer home. "Well, we know where she lives, anyway. Too bad she sensed we were looking at her." Paul decided to chalk that up as a positive.

"So, should we approach her again?"

"No! After last week, we need to give her some time. It looks like more than her boyfriend and her parents know that we approached her at that market."

"Okay. So, just give her some time. You realize we're running out of time to get any more talent signed up, right?"

"Yeah. I know. But she's worth it. I think we should take just a little more time with her. We didn't know something critical about the Amish people and that hurt us. If we're going to succeed in getting her to sign a contestant's contract, we're going to have to slow things down some."

Melody hunched deeper into her warm jacket, grateful for its warmth. She sighed, feeling impatient. "I know you're right. But I also know that Gracie has a ton of natural talent and that it wouldn't take very much to nurture it."

CHAPTER 2

The couple stayed hidden in the trees until long after Abe had left—they weren't interested in him. Instead, they stared at the house, as though it would open up and reveal the information they wanted about Gracie and how to get her to agree to compete in the nationally televised talent competition. Finally, driven away by the deepening cold, they crept out of the trees and snuck back to their car, driving quickly back to Philadelphia to plot and plan some more.

"So, if we just keep approaching her, do you think that'll work? I gotta admit, Paul, I've never encountered resistance like that!" Melody was flummoxed and frustrated by Gracie's stubbornness.

"I am, too. I mean, we only have so many weeks to finish signing up contestants. I'm afraid that, if she doesn't change her mind, we'll have to forget about her." Paul was glum as he drove.

"Paul, no! We have to get her to agree! She'd be one of the best-performing contestants in the show! I mean, think about it. Gaga would adore her voice. So would Harry. I hate to sound trite, but she does have a God-given gift. Maybe we should talk to the producers?"

Paul was silent for several long beats. "I don't know. Look, Melody, think about it. If we tell the producers about her, first they're going to butt in and try to steal her sign-up away from us, if she ever decides to compete. Second, if we go to them and admit that we're having trouble signing up a teenaged contestant? They'd think we've lost our touch and 'bye, Felicia,' there go our jobs. You want that?"

"No, Paul, you know better than that! I'm just trying to think of as many options as I can." Melody retreated back to her own seat, sulking as she turned the heat up in the car. For several minutes, tense silence reigned as both Melody and Paul tried to think of a way to get Gracie Troyer to agree to compete.

Paul sighed. "I'm sorry, Mel. I know you're just as frustrated as I am. I mean, we've never had this kind of trouble before, you know? But we need to think smart, sweetheart! We're salespeople. We sell competition and the possibility of winning 250,000 dollars, plus recording contracts or the chance to perform in New York City. Now, we don't know much about Gracie's cul— Wait a minute. Why didn't we think of that before?"

"What?" Melody had been ready to indulge in a good sulking session, just to teach her husband a lesson. "What are you talking about?"

"We know next to nothing about the Amish, sweetie. Nothing! We need to see what we can find out and see if we can use any of what we learn to help us get that girl signed up. That's what I'm talking about!" Paul was excited.

"Okay, then, when we get up tomorrow, we'll see what we can find out. Before we go to the meeting."

"Yeah, at least we have seven new contestants signed up." If the couple had known even the slightest bit about the Amish "culture," they would have realized right away that contests such as the one they worked on were anathema to the Amish.

The next morning, Melody sat at the computer, Googling everything she could about the Amish, their beliefs and practices. Landing on a scholarly website owned by an anthropology professor in Pennsylvania, she nodded, knowing she would find accurate information. As she read, her face became more and more dejected and she slumped at the computer.

""Hey, what's wrong? You look like you've lost your closest friend!" Paul paused as he moved between the kitchen and living room.

"Crap! Crap, crap, crap!"

"Melody, what is it?"

"Look! I found this guy's website. He's pretty knowledgeable, a professor of anthropology here in Pennsylvania. Here's what he says about the Amish: They can't engage in competition. They follow this German term called 'Gelassenheit,' which means they have to submit to the will of higher authorities. Paul, this means that she won't be allowed to compete! The group's will is more important than individual will." Melody leaned back, threw her hands in the air and sighed in defeat.

Feeling a punch in the gut, Paul leaned over Melody's shoulder and read the website for himself. "Gawd. This is awful. And the way she reacted when we told her we had to sign her up...there's no way she doesn't know this. She's been steeped in it for her whole life! She knows and..." Setting his coffee mug down, Paul muttered several colorful obscenities under his breath. "We gotta think of something. We'll work on this for the next few days. But for now, we need to finish breakfast, clean the kitchen and get to that meeting. If we're not there…"

Melody sighed. She loved the work she and Paul did. They found talented people and helped them to be recognized. But today… "Okay. I've lost my appetite, anyway. I'll put everything in the dishwasher and clean the kitchen. Then we can leave." She was silent on the way to the meeting. During the meeting, she tried to perk up. Listening to the other talent promoters introducing the names of the people they had found for the competition, she did become happier—she and Paul had found contestants who were truly more talented and who had a higher chance of winning the overall competition. When their turn came up to present the peoples' names they had found, she was hopeful. Looking at Paul, she indicated silently to him that he should speak.

Paul cleared his throat and clicked on the first video, introducing the person. Person by person, he introduced them, pointing out their strengths and predicting they would do well in the competition. He sighed and sent an unspoken message to Melody. *I'm going to talk about her even though we don't have a video ready.* "We also came across a teen girl at the Amish market last week. She sings…and man, can she sing! We're working on convincing her that she has a real shot of winning. I think, once we talk more to her parents, we may be able to get her signed up."

"The Amish market? Is she Amish?" The head producer tilted his head and crossed his arms.

"Uh, well… yeah, she is. But—"

"Wait. You can try to get her signed up. But don't hold your breath. I know a little about Amish culture. They don't believe in promoting themselves over others. It's a modesty thing. A thing about pride. You have a real uphill path to getting her or her family to agree, let alone their community. What's her name?"

"All we know is her first name. Gracie." Paul lied outright here, because he didn't want anyone else scooping Gracie Troyer out from under him or Melody.

The producer sighed. "I suppose she sang a hymn, right?"

"Yeah. A hymn. But man, she put some real voice and spirit behind it."

The morning following the sing, Gracie had a hard time shaking off the sense of apprehension she felt. She worked quietly, helping her mamm with the laundry as she prepared her baking.

"Gracie, are you okay?"

"Nee. When Abe was bringing me home last night, I felt like we were being watched. That's why we rushed in here so fast. I don't know what Abe experienced on his way home afterward. But right now, I just feel like there's someone out there watching me."

Abigail shivered. "Daughter, I really wish those people hadn't been there last week!"

"That's why I'm not singing. I don't want them to hear me. I'll sing only in services or here at home from now on." Gracie was solemn and defiant.

"Gut. For now, I think that's an excellent idea. In the meantime, if you're at a stopping point with those cookies, I need help in hanging out the laundry."

Gracie went outside and helped her mamm to hang the sheets and clothing. They flapped wildly in the stiff wind. Grabbing the laundry basket, Gracie hurried back inside, not sure if she needed to worry.

"Did you feel anything, like they were still out there watching you?"

"Nee, not now. I just don't want them to see me anywhere. If I need to buy anything, will you be able to go with me?"

"We'll see. I may be able, depending on what I

have to do. Maybe we can combine your errands with mine."

"That'll work." For several hours, Gracie worked feverishly on her baking—she was finding that she needed to increase production so she could satisfy the needs and wants of everyone who visited the market every week.

That night, Abe came by. "Do you have time for a short buggy ride?"

Gracie was apprehensive. "Can we stay just around here? After last night, I'm just scared."

"Ya. I understand. Get your coat because it's cold and windy out here."

In the buggy, Gracie hugged her arms around her, staving off the cold and praying that whoever had been out there the night before was far away.

"So, I wanted to let you know that while I was driving home, I may have gotten the same creepy feeling you did on the way home from the sing." Abe was tentative, a rare situation for him.

"*May have* gotten the same feeling?" Gracie was confused.

Abe shifted uncomfortably on the seat. "Ya. I got a creepy feeling, like someone was just *spying* on me."

Gracie gasped and turned toward Abe. "No! Take me back home! Please!"

"Wait. Slow down, Gracie. Do you feel that same sensation right now? Think."

Letting down a shaky breath, Gracie clasped her hands together. Shaking her head, she spoke. "Nee. But that doesn't mean—"

"Gracie, my liebe, what it means is that whoever it was isn't here today. They left. When I got that feeling last night, I stopped my buggy and stood up. I looked all around and I made it obvious that I was doing so. I was about to shout at them, when I heard at least one set of footsteps just crunching through the underbrush, just running away. Gracie, I scared them by letting them know that I knew they were out there."

"Who?"

"Probably that couple that confronted you last week."

Gracie's eyes rounded and she gasped again. "No! Why won't they leave me alone? I told them I didn't want to!"

"Gracie, they don't want to take 'no' for an answer. I think we need to talk to our parents, then to the deacon."

Gracie looked around, worry on her delicate features. "Abe, if we're going anywhere, can we get there, please? Soon?"

"How about the diner? We can have coffee or hot chocolate while we talk about what to do."

"That's gut. Ya, let's go there." Even though Gracie didn't feel like they were being spied on, she knew she wouldn't be completely comfortable until they were off the road. Once inside, she released a long sigh of relief.

"What'll you two have?" The waitress held her pen over her order pad. She was bored, her feet hurt and all she wanted was to be at home, watching television.

"We'll both have hot chocolate and apple pie, please."

"Comin' up." The waitress walked off.

A few minutes later, Abe dug into his dessert. "So, here's what I was thinking. We go talk to our parents and to Deacon Bontrager. Ask him to tell both ministers. You start telling all your friends what happened and what these people are still doing. I'll do the same with my friends. Make sure you tell your brothers and sisters as well. I want these people to see that you have all kinds of support surrounding you. And that you're not going to...wait, do you want to take part in this show?" Abe held his breath, waiting for Gracie's answer.

"Nee! Of course not! I want them to stop bothering me, period!"

Abe let out a deep breath of relief. "Thank Gott!"

"Your idea is a gut one, Abe. All day long today, I just felt...*weird*. Like there was something just holding me down. And I told mamm that I wasn't going to sing in public anymore."

"What did she say?"

"It's a gut idea. I'm also going to combine my shopping errands with hers, so we can be out at the same time. Just in case."

"Also an excellent idea. About not singing in public. I can understand why you don't want to anymore, but..."

"I just don't want them to hear me. At all!" Gracie shivered, holding her arms around her middle.

Abe put his hand on the table, beckoning Gracie to put one of her hands into his. "I would miss your singing in public. But I see exactly where you're coming from. You feel—this is just a guess—but you feel like this gift is being stolen from you."

"Ya, exactly. That's exactly how I feel."

Before they left to go back home, Abe reminded Gracie what they'd decided. "We'll tell everyone what happened—though I can't see how everybody doesn't know this already. If they decide to come back, it would be gut if you can be with your parents. If they can't be with you, then be with several of your friends. I know you're worried about them, liebe, but if you could let them know that you aren't going to change your mind, that might take some of the pressure off you."

Settling into the buggy, Gracie relaxed, feeling tears threatening to fall. "That's perfect, Abe. One thing, though. *I* need to be able to be the one to tell them. Otherwise, they'll feel like they can keep bugging me. Because they'll think that the elders, or my parents—or even you—are making me do so."

Abe was well acquainted with Gracie's independence. "I know. And I agree. I wonder…if you hadn't been born Amish, would you have reacted the same way?"

This was a question Gracie hadn't expected. Stunned into silence, she stared into the distance, just wondering.

"Gracie?"

"I…I don't know. I suppose, if I'd grown up around all the supplies and equipment that an Englisch singer is used to, along with the traditions of pride, ambition and competitiveness, I probably would have jumped at the chance." Gracie's voice faded away as she considered the question. "I just don't know. I do know this. I am grateful to have been born Amish." Her voice firmed up and she sounded like her usual, confident self.

Abe grinned, feeling relief. "I'm sorry. I just needed to know."

"I understand, Abe."

৹৵৵

I n Philadelphia, Melody slumped into a comfortable armchair after she and Paul came back home. She was still just as dejected as she was when they went to their meeting. "What...a...day!"

CHAPTER 3

"Yeah, I agree. I think we should go back to Crawford County. I want to see if we can find this girl and convince her."

"I would love to. But after what we read on that website this morning, she's going to have the backing of her parents, friends and the preachers, priests or whatever they're called in the Amish world."

"Hmmm. Maybe. But maybe we can work on her and get her to agree?"

Melody thought about it. "Maybe. But I just want one night without thinking about that show."

That caught Paul's attention. He heard the frustration in Melody's voice. Looking closely at her, he saw that she was feeling a physical result of their recent struggle to get Gracie Troyer's agreement to compete.

Melody was leaned over, facing the floor. She was slowly massaging her temples.

"You okay?"

"Do I look okay?"

Paul recoiled, hearing the edge of anger in Melody's voice. "Okay. We'll back off on this girl. Won't talk about her tonight. But at some point, we do need to come up with some ideas. Because she would be the perfect contestant for *The Country's Most Talented*.

"Okay, whatevs. Just… Not tonight!" Jumping to her feet, Melody strode into the kitchen. Pulling a wine glass from the cabinet, she opened a bottle of wine and poured a generous serving.

Paul, seeing her, judiciously decided he should back off. Closing his mouth, he pulled two small steaks from the refrigerator and tossed them on their outdoor grill. As they cooked, he pulled microwavable twice-baked potatoes and frozen vegetables from the freezer. "Dinner's ready."

"Thanks." Melody ate and poured a second glass of wine. "Want a glass?"

"Nah. I think I'll have a beer instead tonight." After cleaning the kitchen, Paul came into the brightly lit living room. Seeing that Melody was focused on her current crochet project, he relaxed. *Good. Maybe she'll feel better in the morning.* At his computer, he put earbuds in his ears so he could watch and listen to videos of current contestants. Silence reigned as each worked on their evening's projects.

That evening, Gracie was walking outside, just thinking about her situation. As she did so, she felt like singing so she could pray about the issue confronting her. About to open her mouth and sing a hymn, she remembered her promise to her mamm just in time. Instead, she retreated to the yard, where she plopped onto the porch swing just outside the kitchen. *Gott, I don't know what to do! Singing is such a big part of my life, and now I feel like I can't even sing outside anymore! I'm afraid of being out in public by myself, just in case they're here in Crawford County. I don't want them here! I don't want to be on that TV show. Gott, please help me find a way to deal with them.* Feeling slightly better, Gracie went into the house. Shivering slightly, she heated water for hot tea.

That weekend, the rumspringe youth went to Lancaster to go see a movie. Sitting in the theater with popcorn and sodas, everyone felt relaxed. Gracie felt gloriously anonymous. She giggled at the funny parts of the movie and sniffled at the sad parts. Riding home in Stephen's car, she felt relatively safe. As they waited at a stoplight, she looked out the rear passenger window and gasped. Paul was looking right at her and smiling! "Stephen! Go! Now!"

"Why? I still have the...okay, now I can go." Stomping hard on the gas pedal, Stephen peeled away from the intersection. "What was it?"

"That Mister Wilson. He was in the car next to yours! He saw me!"

Abe let out a very rare imprecation. "Gott, no!" He turned his body in the back seat, looking to see if he could spot Paul's car. "I don't see him. Just get us back home, please." He wrapped his arm around Gracie's suddenly tensed shoulders. "Calm down, liebe. Stephen's an excellent driver."

In the front seat, Stephen was watching the road and taking turns as fast as he dared. As he entered the Amish area of Crawford County, he heaved out a noisy sigh of relief. "Why don't we stop at my house for a while?" Abe and I can watch the road to see if we spot those people. Abe, why don't you stand outside with Gracie while she tries to get her parents on the phone? That way, they'll know she's back in the community, but delayed because of those people."

"Ya, excellent idea."

Gracie quickly made her call, promising to be back home as soon as they all knew the Wilsons wouldn't be trying to find and harass her. Inside the Zook home, the youth drank hot coffee and peered out the window. After nearly an hour had passed, they decided the Wilsons weren't going to drive by.

"I'm taking her home now. We both have work to do tomorrow and it's getting late." Abe gave Stephen a grateful grin and quickly escorted Gracie out. He drove her home as fast as he could. Sitting next to him, Gracie felt like her eyes were protruding from her head as she looked all around her, trying to find the Wilsons. Riding into the front yard she felt a headache beginning to develop.

"You okay?"

"Nee. I'm scared and angry. I also have a headache." Gracie was livid. As Abe kissed her, she tried to relax, but she couldn't. "I'm sorry, I just can't relax."

"Don't worry. Get inside and we'll hang out tomorrow evening." Abe watched carefully as Gracie hurried to the front door and inside. Just as she closed the front door, he saw headlights slowly approaching the house. Feeling hot anger boiling inside him, Abe waited for the car to stop just outside the fence line.

"Hey, is this where Gracie lives?"

"Why?"

Paul looked inside at Melody. He hadn't expected the anger or hostility from an Amish teen. "Uh, we want to talk to her?"

"She doesn't want to talk to you. She's pretty upset right now."

"Listen. I don't know who you are. But we did some research about the Amish. We know there are rules against competition, but we're trying to find out if there's any way that—"

"No! There is no way! Now leave!" Abe yelled as loudly as he could—he had just heard what Paul couldn't: horse's hooves approaching the Troyer property. With relief, he heard the pace of the hooves picking up.

"Abe Lapp? Is that you?"

"Ya, deacon. I just dropped Gracie off after a date. We were in Lancaster to go see a movie."

"Huh. And who are these people?" The deacon indicated the Wilsons with a sweep of his hand.

"These are the people harassing poor Gracie

about joining their mupsich competition." All the disdain and disgust that Abe felt dripped off his words. He tried to relax, feeling his tension in the tightened muscles of his back.

The deacon jumped from his buggy and tied the reins to the fence railing. Next, he walked slowly to the opened driver's door of the car. "Deacon Eli Bontrager. Who do I have the...*pleasure*...of speaking to?"

Paul shifted on his feet. He felt tension seeping into his body. His voice was tight. "Paul Wilson. My wife is in the car as well. She...we heard Gracie singing a couple weeks ago. She has a gorgeous voice, one that is just what we're looking for in amateurs. For, uh, the TV show, *The Country's Most Talented*."

"Hmmm. I remember your encounter with Gracie; she told you straight out why she couldn't accept your offer. Yet you continue to follow and harass her. I would agree with Abe here. You are harassing her. Abe, tell me, how did she realize she'd been spotted again?"

Abe explained the sequence of events. "We were in Stephen's car. Gracie and I were in the back seat and she looked over. She recognized him because he was looking straight at her. She gasped and told Stephen to go, so he did. When I got her home a minute ago, she was angry and said she had gotten a headache. And now, I'm right angry myself."

"And justifiably so. Mister Wilson, is it? Ya, we know who you and your wife are. For now, I am the spiritual head of the Crawford County community here. And I strongly suggest you leave here. And never come back. Gracie was right to respond as she did last week. We don't believe in bringing attention or glory to ourselves. It goes against what the Bible tells us to do, which is to be modest and plain in our appearances and actions. For Gracie to compete in your show, she would violate that practice. She would also violate our Ordnung. Even though she hasn't been baptized yet, she knows what the Ordnung tells us to do—"

"Sir? What is the 'Ordnung?'" Paul was genuinely confused.

Abe let out a loud guffaw. "Hah! You didn't research us well enough!"

"Abe, let me handle this, please." The deacon's voice was deceptively calm as his eyes blazed with anger. "Mister Wilson, our Ordnung is an unwritten, but well-known, set of rules that governs every member of our community. If you are researching our beliefs and practices, I would strongly suggest that you study what the Ordnung is and how it structures our community's life. Now, I am telling you once again—leave here. And, if I hear that you have continued to bother Gracie, I will bring in the bishop of an adjoining community to help protect her." Silently, he moved, standing shoulder-to-shoulder with Abe, presenting a united line of defense in front of Gracie. Both Amishmen felt tendrils of physical tension tightening up their shoulders, abdomens and backs. Abe spread his feet wide and settled his hands on his lean hips, making himself seem bigger.

Paul, seeing this, admitted defeat in his mind. Sighing and rolling his eyes, he slipped back into his car. Looking silently at both men with a glower on his face, he put the small car into gear and took off.

"Abe, do you have many work plans tomorrow?"

"Ya, I need to go make deliveries to some customers. Why?"

"You're not working on any pieces? Because I'm thinking that you, me and a few other men should stay here through the night, ensuring that the Wilsons won't be back to bother Miss Troyer."

"Gut idea. But I'd have to let daed know."

"Done. I'll go tell him for you if you'll let Mister Troyer know what we're doing tonight. I'm thinking I can get a few other men and teen boys here as well so we can take it in shifts. This way, we don't need to lose the whole night and we can get some sleep."

"Denki. Ya, I'll go tell him. If you'd ask my daed for my sleeping bag, that'll keep the night's cold off."

"Excellent plan. I'll see you in a little while." The deacon drove off fast. After telling Ben Lapp what was happening, he slung Abe's sleeping bag into his buggy. Less than one hour later, he led a caravan of buggies back to the Troyer home. "Abe, Jon, I brought seven other men back with me. I figure we can all take one-hour shifts overnight."

"Denki. Abigail made several pots of coffee and filled some thermoses so we can stay awake for our shifts. It looks like everyone brought something to sleep in until their shift comes up. Let's decide on who will be guarding the house when." Shift assignments were quickly decided upon and the men discussed whether to stay in the front yard or walk around.

"We should walk around the whole property. I don't trust the Wilsons. They're sneaky and stubborn." Abe was sober as he spoke.

"Gut point. Then, I'll get started. The rest of you should sleep. Jon, how is Gracie?"

"Scared and madder than a cat whose paw got stepped on."

Everyone dispersed, leaving Eli Bontrager to walk slowly around the large Troyer property. His hour passed uneventfully and he was grateful for the hot coffee and his warm coat. His hour-long shift passed quietly and he was relieved by Jon Troyer. "It's all quiet, Jon. I pray it's just as quiet for you."

"Denki. Go sleep."

Jon's shift, as well as Abe's and Stephen's, were all quiet. Shortly after Minister Dan Summy started his shift, he heard the low rumble of an engine driving very slowly down the road. Alerted, he crept quickly, but quietly to the side of the Troyer house. Looking at the other men, he saw a few heads raised from their sleeping bags. "Jon. Deacon, I hear a car engine."

Jon and Eli slipped out of their sleeping bags and crawled over toward Dan. They were soon joined by the remaining men.

"South of here, coming from PA 408 West. "

All heads swiveled as one, homing in on the sound of a car's engine slowly approaching the property. The car came to a stop, not seeing all the men gathered in a clump, at the side of the house.

The deacon started walking quickly toward the Subaru. The rest of the men followed. "Mr. Wilson. We meet again! What are you doing here at this time of the night? Or should I say morning?"

Paul Wilson couldn't speak. He was too transfixed by the sight of seven somber-faced Amishmen confronting him. "Ahh...I..."

"Can't speak, can you? Maybe you should get it into your brain that my daughter said no to you because, oh, maybe, she doesn't want to take part in your show?"

Paul grabbed onto one inaccuracy. "It's not my show. It's—"

"We don't care. What we do care about is that you are here, not five hours after my daughter's boyfriend told you to leave! Now, we aren't always open to involving the sheriff in our matters. But we can at least think about it."

Paul's face suddenly looked sickly-white under the tan he'd obtained. "No, please. That won't be necessary. I'll leave her alone."

Deacon Bontrager caught on to the omission. "Ach. So, you'll leave her alone. But your wife won't?"

"No! No, that's not what I meant! Not at all! She'll leave her alone, too. I-I just left her out because she's not here. I couldn't sleep. So I drove here from Philly just so I could, you know, think…" Slowly, Paul's voice trailed away, as though aware that his rationalizations were weak, at best. "Maybe I should just leave."

"Excellent idea. Another wunderbaar idea is that you just don't come back. Ever." Abe's voice was a low, angered rumble.

Putting his car back into gear, Paul hurriedly left.

The men all stood around, watching the red tail-lights growing smaller and smaller until they finally vanished. The deacon broke the tense silence. "So. Do we stay here, just in case? Or go home?"

CHAPTER 4

"Deacon, if you don't mind the temporary discomforts of hard ground and a cold night, I...*we* would be grateful if all of you would stay. I don't trust that Paul Wilson any more than I could fling my biggest horse."

The mental image had all the men chuckling to relieve the physical and emotional tension that had built up.

"That's settled, then. Let's all go to sleep. I think we may have frightened Mister Wilson off. For the moment at least. If anyone hears anything, speak up!"

Lying in his bag, Abe found that he had a hard time getting to sleep. He was having a hard time allowing his body to dispel the accumulated anger and mental tension. Feeling growing pain in his neck and shoulders, he flexed them, and then decided to get up. He moved as quietly as he could so he wouldn't wake anyone up. Snugging his coat more closely around his torso, he walked around, just paying attention to everything he heard and saw going on around him. Standing in between the shadows of two broad bushes, he watched up and down the road fronting the Troyer home. If he squinted, he was able to see clear to both roads at the ends of Rosebush Lane. Aside from two or three large, lumbering and slow-moving vehicles, nothing else came near either intersection. Finally, Abe felt himself growing powerful sleepy. Muffling his yawn, he returned to a cold sleeping bag.

❦

Back in his high-rise apartment, Paul paced back and forth in his and Melody's study. He'd closed the door so he could turn on the desk lamp. As he paced, he swore colorfully, calling down all sorts of painful imprecations on the male residents of the Crawford County Amish community. He wanted Gracie on the show! "And I'm going to do everything it takes to get her to say she will. Anything!" Dropping down into his squeaky office chair, Paul buried his chin in his hand

and began to think of anything he could do to induce Gracie to agree to their request.

Finally, he did what he should have done from the beginning—he cracked open one of the library books he and Melody had checked out. Ten minutes later, he was engrossed in the words. Looking up "Ordnung," he learned about this unwritten institution. *So, it looks like these are regulations that everyone has to follow. If they don't, baptized members can be visited by the elders—given what that deacon made me feel like, that's not a pleasant prospect. If they deliberately disobey these regulations, wow! They can be banned. Holy...that sounds like excommunication to me.* Reading that Amish residents simply "knew" what their community's Ordnung contained, Paul shook his head, perplexed. *Does this mean the little kids know it as well? How?* Leaning back, Paul thought. *I wonder if Gracie's been baptized yet. And if her status affects whether she can participate without danger of being kicked out.* Finally, Paul yawned widely. Looking at the atomic clock hanging on the wall, he closed the book and went to bed. As he slept, he dreamed about his scary encounter with the Amishmen.

Paul looked at Melody with a wide grin. "I got her to agree! She's in the show!"

Melody squealed with excitement. "How?"

"I found a loophole in this Ordnung that regulates what their community can do or not do."

"Ooooh, do tell." Melody's voice dropped into a low register that made Paul's heart pound.

"Uh, yeah. As it turns out, because she's not baptized yet, she's not held to the same standards as the adults in Crawford County."

"And?"

"This means that, before she's baptized or married, she can take part in certain activities without the danger of excommunication. Or what they call 'the ban.' So, we have her as a contestant!"

Paul woke up suddenly, gasping. He squeezed his eyes shut against the brightness coming from the window.

"Hey! You slept later than normal. It's a good thing you're awake. We have a meeting in about an hour and a half."

"Crap! Why didn't you wake me earlier?" Paul threw the warm blankets back, grateful he'd put on sleep pants.

"Well, you got to bed after three in the morning. What were you doing?"

"Melody, I hope the coffee is hot. Because I gotta story for you." Hurrying to the kitchen, Paul toasted an English muffin and poured a tall mug of coffee.

"First, I went back to Crawford County. It was about two this morning when I got—"

"What? You did *what*? I didn't like how that bishop, priest, deacon, whatever he is, was talking to you!"

"I know. I know. But I wasn't thinking clearly. I need to finish before we get ready and go to the office. So, I got back to the street they live on. It was all quiet and dark. Next thing I know, I'm in front of their house and there's like, seven or eight Amishmen standing around the car. Gracie's dad got sarcastic on me, and then her boyfriend just told me to make myself scarce. Then that deacon guy told me that, even though they don't like to get the cops involved in their business, they would if they had to. Jeebus, Melody, that made me stop right there! I left, fast! When I got back here, I was still too wired to go to sleep. So I decided to do a little studying. I looked up that Ordnung thing in one of the books we checked out. Melody, it's an unwritten set of regulations that everyone just seems to learn by osmosis. It's not written. And, if they go against any one of those regulations, well, the person can be excommunicated and can't have any contact with anyone in the community."

"Holy…" Melody paused, unable to go any further. "I don't want to do that to her!"

"Neither do I."

"So, what do we do, Paul?"

"We find out if someone her age, who's still not baptized, is held to the same regulations as those who have been baptized."

Melody's eyes rounded and she gasped. "You mean…?"

"That's part of why I overslept." Paul paused, starting another cup of coffee in the Keurig coffee maker. "I had a dream, probably stimulated by what happened last night. In that dream, I told you about this loophole. Because she hasn't been baptized, she may be able to agree to compete! We just need to find out if that's true or not."

Melody was unable to speak. She just looked at Paul, excitement growing in her eyes. "You mean we may actually be able to get her to agree to compete?" Her voice slid into a much higher register as she finished asking her question.

"It's just a possibility. And we need to find out for sure whether that's true or not. So, let's try to go slow here."

In response, Melody dragged a deep breath in through her nose and exhaled slowly.

Going to the meeting, they mutually agreed they wouldn't say anything about Gracie.

Deacon Eli sat in his kitchen, drinking a hot cup of coffee. His face betrayed the worry and tension roiling his spirit. He was thinking of Gracie Troyer. *If she was only older than sixteen! If she were nearing baptism or, ideally, already baptized, we wouldn't have to worry so much about this couple. As it is now, she's actively in her rumspringa. She can legally try out new experiences— such as recording songs for music albums. Compete in this show, if she decides she wants to do so.* Eli was troubled. Should he tell her or her family, or keep this information to himself? He knew the repercussions that would rock the community if he did tell them that Gracie could, conceivably, agree to take part in the television show. *Even though she's not taking baptismal instruction, by agreeing to take part in this show, she would violate our standards on bringing attention to herself. She might even begin to feel pride in the talent that God has given to her. Nee. I won't say anything. No need to put her at risk or set that temptation in front of her.* Finishing his coffee, he felt more relaxed and at peace. Knowing how much work he needed to get done, he called out to his wife where he'd be.

At home, Gracie felt comfortable, but only when she was inside and not facing a trip to the store. She was thankful that today she and her mamm would be going to the store together. Looking up at a knock on the door, Gracie tensed up. She didn't want to open it, just in case one of the Wilsons was on the porch. The knock sounded once again.

"Gracie, aren't you going to get that?" Abigail brushed past her and paused as she saw Gracie's tensed-up shoulders. "What's wrong?"

"I'm afraid it might be the Wilsons."

"Only one way to find out, right?" Abigail opened the door as though she had no worries. A wide smile creased her face. "Miriam! How are you, child?"

"Gut! I was wondering if you and Gracie would like someone to come with you shopping today. I have a lot of things to buy!"

Come in! Ya! Gracie, it's Miriam." Abigail's voice held a strong note of relief. She had been afraid as well.

Gracie let out the big breath she'd been holding. "Oh, Miriam! Thank Gott it's you!"

"Why? Oh, you're afraid it's one of the Wilsons, right? No worries. I saw several men and teen boys just watching the roads in and out of the community. If anyone sees their car, they'll make them leave." Miriam snapped her fingers. "Like that!"

Gracie wanted to cry at the kindness and love

being displayed by everyone. Clearing her throat, she spoke. "I need to thank everyone."

※

At the store, Gracie, her mamm and Miriam loaded their carts with the items they needed. Gracie felt more relaxed. Yet she knew that because the store was owned by an Englisch company, the Wilsons could come in at any time. And she didn't know if she would have any ability to make them leave her alone. It was because of this that, as the moments slipped by, she began displaying more and more tension. By the time all three women were waiting in line to pay for their items, she had developed a throbbing headache at the back of her head and her neck felt as hard as a brick wall.

"Daughter, what is wrong? Are you sick?"

"Nee. Headache, and my neck is so stiff." Gracie grimaced as she tried to turn her head and make her neck relax.

"Gracie, are you worried that they'll come in here?"

"Y-ya." Gracie was unable to look around and see if the Wilsons had come in. She sighed. "I just want to pay and get home. Fast."

As it turned out, the Wilsons were in the area. Gracie's tears were justified. As she, Abigail and Miriam walked out of the store to put their bags into the buggy, Melody Wilson jogged toward them. "Gracie!"

"Mamm! We have to go, now!" Gracie and Miriam threw the rest of the bags into the buggy, willy-nilly, then clambered in, not caring that they were exposing the length of their legs.

"Girlie, Boy, hurry!" Abigail whipped the reins on the horses' backs. The horses responded fast, jumping into an immediate canter, then a trot as they reached a more open area. As they reached the open road, the horses sped up into a full gallop, their hooves eating up the distance and leaving the intruders far behind.

"Gracie! All we want..." Melody's words faded into nothingness.

Gracie slowly began to relax as she sensed they were leaving the Wilsons far in the distance. She tried turning her head, grimacing as the tenseness in her neck pinged.

"Don't. I'll look." Miriam gripped Gracie's wrist in one hand, turning and looking behind them. "Thank Gott. They are way back there. But Missus Troyer, we need to keep moving."

"Ya. I have experience with making our horses

move fast." Abigail spoke through her teeth, holding onto the reins as tightly as she could. Seeing a turn-off up ahead, she signaled the horses to slow for the turn. The buggy made the turn, with two wheels almost leaving the road. "Okay, nearly home. Just keep going!"

The horses kept moving, knowing that their mistress' worry was still present. Because the day was so cold, they didn't overheat, but they were at risk of becoming exhausted. "Miriam, do you see their car?"

Miriam twisted around again. "Nee. We took off pretty fast."

"Girlie, Boy, slow down, whoa, whoa." In response, the horses slowed into a canter. They blew out noisy breaths as they tried to regulate their breathing. Abigail knew that not many Englischers were aware of this little side road. Keeping the horses at a gentle walk, she sighed. "Thank Gott we all moved so fast. I'm going to go and talk to the deacon after we get home. Gracie, I want you to put things away. Miriam, I'll take you home right now."

"Mammmm, I don't want to be at home alone!" Gracie's voice was full of fear.

"Your daed will be in the barn. We'll tell him what happened. You know, you're right. We'll put the perishables away, and then go talk to Deacon

Bontrager. All of us. Miriam, do you mind going with us?"

"Nee, that's fine. I can tell Mamm what happened when I get home. She already knows. Everyone here does."

Arriving at home, Gracie and Miriam put the perishables into the freezer and refrigerator as Abigail hurried to the barn to tell Jon what had happened.

"All of us are going to talk to the deacon."

"Gut idea, wife." Jon dusted his hands off. In the house, he washed his dusty face clean. "Ready?"

"U nfortunately, we have no way of controlling who goes into an Englisch store. Were you unable to find what you needed in our store?"

"Nee. We needed a few things that our store doesn't have." Abigail was calm once again, feeling that she could shift the problem to the deacon's shoulders.

Eli sighed. "We're stuck with them until they get the message that she cannot participate in that contest. I'm going to go to an adjoining community and consult with their bishop to find out what else we can do, if anything."

Everyone looked at Gracie. "Please! I know we're limited in what we can do. But I just want to know if there's a way I can make them stop approaching me."

CHAPTER 5

"Unfortunately, nothing short of a restraining order." Eli had some knowledge of this legal remedy.

"A what?" Gracie was ferhoodled.

"Restraining order. It's a legal order that Englischers use to keep people from harassing them."

Jon grinned. "But do the Wilsons know this? If they know so little about our beliefs and culture..."

The deacon looked long and hard at Jon, his mouth slightly open. "Huh! Gut idea! Gracie, when they do approach you, and they will, tell them that if they don't stop, you're going to go to the courthouse —don't say anything about the Englisch courthouse —just say 'courthouse' and let them know you're ready to get a restraining order. And tell them that if they keep bugging you, you're going to have them put in jail."

Now, it was Gracie's mouth that hung open. Then, she grinned. "Ya! Okay, I will. I like that!" Needing to expend a little excess energy, she began to skip around the kitchen, giggling.

"Gracie. Because we don't yet have a bishop selected for our community, I'm going to go see a bishop in another community. I can guide you and point you to different portions of our Ordnung, but this situation is a bit beyond my ability to fully help you get rid of these people. I know enough to say that I don't have all the knowledge I need. I believe I've heard the Englisch call it 'beyond my pay grade.'"

Once again, Gracie was confused. "That sounds like…like someone who says the decision is something their boss should make. Am I right?"

"Ya, exactly! I don't feel like I have enough experience with our flock here to be able to help you effectively. It's in times like this that I truly feel my lack of knowledge. I'll be leaving early tomorrow morning and I'll speak to a nearby bishop. I pray that I'll be able to gain more knowledge. Gracie, do you mind if I explain your situation to the bishop?"

"Nee, go ahead. I feel like you've been very effective. But if you feel more comfortable calling on a bishop, it's fine with me."

Gracie smiled. "I feel so much better now. Denki."

Back in her car, Melody swore to herself. A passing Amishwoman overheard the swear words and glared at Melody. "Ma'am, I am only thankful that my kinder are with their grandmother right now! Restrain yourself!"

"Sorry. I'm just so frustrated!"

The Amishwoman gasped. "You're that woman that's trying to get our Gracie into your program! On television! Leave here and don't come back."

Melody, seeing the look of disdain on the other woman's face, started her car and, barely looking around her, peeled out, heading for the expressway.

The Amishwoman coughed and glared after Melody's quickly retreating car.

As Melody drove, she fumed. The occasional swear word left her mouth. She had remembered to close her windows so nobody else could hear what she was saying. Every so often, as she continued to think of her failed attempt to contact Gracie yet again, another swear word would pop out. Slowly, she grew more dispirited as she thought of the shortening deadline to have contestants signed up for the nationally televised competition. At home, she slumped uncharacteristically in the recliner, barely acknowledging Paul when he came in.

"Hey, what's wrong?"

"Who else?"

"*Who* else? Don't you mean *what* else?"

Once again, Melody began to swear, long and loud. She finished with, "And I spotted her coming out of the store! She and her mother had bought a bunch of baking things. I called her name. They panicked and threw their things into their wagon or whatever it is. And took off! I was in my car and I swore a little bit. One of those Amish women was passing by my car and she pretended to be shocked at my vulgarity. She had the nerve to tell me to restrain myself! And she said she 'thanked God' that her kids were with their grandmother while she shopped!"

"So, she got away again. And she was with her mother." Paul now swore. "I think she's going to be pretty cautious from now on, by being with a family member whenever she's out in public."

Melody whimpered as she fell back into the recliner. "Why did we have to hear her singing? Why—?"

"Did she have to be born Amish, is more like it.

We are going to have the worst time getting to her without any of her family or relatives around. Or more to the point, those bearded priests or whatever they're called."

"What are we going to do? How do we get to her?"

"First, we still have a few months to sign her. We're just going to keep everything about her on the down-low. And—"

"But you talked about her in the last meeting!"

"Yeah, well, I'm going to tell the producer that there's no way she'll be able to participate because of her church's rules."

"But that doesn't get us any closer to getting her!"

"Wait, Melody. I've thought this out."

Melody shot a suspicious look at Paul. "Okay. Well, spill it!"

"Finally! Okay, I'm going to tell the producer in our next meeting that the priest or whatever took me aside and let me have it. That he told me that if we ever showed our faces there in the Crawford County community, they would not hesitate in calling the sheriff. Y'know, that will make the other promoters hesitate to go there and take her out from under us. In the meantime, we'll stay away for several weeks. 'Cuz, we do have some time, remember. After a good amount of time has passed, we'll slide back over and see if we can find her and convince her."

Melody was silent, holding her lower lip between her teeth as she thought. "Okay. That could work. Because, if she...if the whole community thinks we've given up, they'll let their guard down. When it is, we can go right back in and start working on her."

"And on that priest of theirs."

"Yeah! I like it. Let's go for it. How are you going to convince the manager and everyone else that we were threatened with legal action?"

"Pull off the biggest acting job of my life!"

I n Crawford County, Gracie continued to act cautiously, refusing to sing in public. She steadfastly refused to go out in public by herself, absolutely convinced that the Wilsons were still out there, waiting for just the right moment to pounce, isolate her and convince her to take part in their competition.

One morning, Gracie came down to the kitchen, to find it dark and still. "Mamm? Where are you?" Turning, she sped back upstairs and hurried toward her parents' bedroom. There, she found Abigail lying bundled up under the heavy blanket and quilt. "Mamm? What's wrong?"

"Oh, daughter, I'm so sorry! I'm sick. I've been in the bathroom, vomiting all night long."

"Oh, no! Do you want some water? Or ginger tea? How about some dry toast?"

Abigail wrinkled her face at the mention of toast. "Mmmmm, nee! All I can handle is fluids."

"I'll be back upstairs with the tea and a glass of water. Just sip on them! And I'll check on you as well. Where's Daed?"

"In the barn, feeding the livestock. Daughter, there's no way I can go to the store with you. I'm just too sick. And I'd make others around me sick, including you."

"Okay. I'll be back with the tea." Whirling around, Gracie hurried back downstairs and began to boil the water for the promised tea. Pouring the boiling water over the root, she began to cook the bacon and whip the eggs for scrambled eggs. The coffee had just finished perking when Jon came in.

"You know your mamm is sick, right? She can't go anywhere."

"She told me. I won't go to town by myself, so I'll wait until she's...oh, no. I can't go tomorrow. I have to be at the market all day long tomorrow."

"Can you wait to buy what you need? If so, then that's just what you'll have to do."

Gracie wrung her hands together. "I can wait. I have enough baking goods today to finish baking what I need to make. Daed, will I be safe at the market tomorrow?"

"I believe you will be. But I talked to your uncle. He will be sending your older cousin here to help you out. Molly will stay here tonight and spend all day tomorrow at the market with you. Then, your uncle will come over and pick her up to take her home."

Gracie didn't often show physical affection to her family, but today she did. Rushing toward Jon and throwing her arms around his middle, she exclaimed, "Daed, denki!"

For the rest of the day, Gracie alternated between taking tea and water to Abigail. Downstairs, she washed her hands well and baked.

"Gracie, I'm feeling just a little hungry. We have some crackers in the pantry, if you'd bring a few to me, please."

"Okay, but be cautious. Do you think this is a stomach flu, or…"

"Ya. That's what it is. I won't burden you with the details." The Amish rarely went into detail about bodily functions, so Gracie accepted her mother's decision. "I was feeling a little unsettled when I went to sleep last night. Then, I spent most of the night in the restroom. After resting my stomach all day long, I've been able to hold down fluids. I'll see what happens with one cracker and go from there. I'll let you know what happens."

"Okay, I'll be upstairs in a few minutes, then." Gracie hurried downstairs and checked on the status of the cake she was baking, satisfied that she had time to take the crackers up to her mamm before having to remove the cake from the oven. After taking a small plate upstairs, Gracie washed her hands, feeling like she'd washed them at least one hundred times that day. She began to mix the glaze for the cake. Hearing the timer ding, she grabbed the potholders and carefully removed the cake from the oven.

Letting the cake cool, Gracie hummed and sang in the kitchen, letting the full glory of her voice ring out. Remembering what had happened to her a few weeks earlier, she stopped and checked the doors and windows. Assured that they were securely locked, she continued, feeling her spirit right itself in Gott's love and support. Remembering her mamm, she hurried upstairs again. "Mamm, how do you feel?"

"My stomach is crampy, but not like last night. I

still have my tea here. I feel stronger, so I'll make myself more tea when I need it."

"Thank Gott. We have mint leaves if you want to make mint tea."

"Ya, I think that would help with the cramping. How is your baking coming along?"

"I'm nearly done. The cake is cooling and the glaze is ready. Then, I'll wash up, make supper and wait for Molly to come. She'll take your place tomorrow so you can rest and get well."

"So, she will be here. Gut. Maybe, if I'm well, we can go shopping on Saturday. Does that work well for you?"

"Ya, it does. I'm just glad Sunday isn't a meeting Sunday."

Putting her hand over her mouth, Abigail burped, and then sighed in relief.

"I bet that helped." Gracie grinned.

"Much better. I'll be downstairs in a while."

"Okay. I hope you keep getting better." Gracie hurried downstairs.

The next day, Gracie nervously blew a long breath through her pursed lips. She was nervous, even with her older cousin, Molly, by her side. Carrying containers to the buggy, she stashed them in the back, on the seat and floor. By the time she and Molly finished, she had containers stacked on the floor and level with the back seat. The containers on the back seat were level with the windows of the buggy. "Ready?"

"Ya. Also, would you please fill me in on this Englischer couple? What they look like, their name and what they tried to do to you so far."

"Ya, I'm happy to do that. Their name is Wilson. Mister Wilson has brown hair and he dresses like some rich Englischer. He has one of these little..." Gracie waved her hand around. "I don't know, patches of hair just under his lower lip."

"Ah, I think they call those 'soul patches.'" Molly squinted as she tried to remember the term.

Gracie giggled. "He needs a soul and he needs to leave me alone! He's sort of tall and slender. But not like he works outdoors. Missus Wilson has reddish hair and she's pretty. She wears makeup and jewelry. I suppose her clothes are stylish. And both of them are aggressive! 'Please sing for us! Oh, we have to sign you up for our competition show.' I told them nee and ran."

"Ooooh! That's bad! I hope you told them about the Ordnung."

"Ya. I did. So did our deacon. He has been wunderbaar. He's talking to a bishop in another community about how else we can stop the Wilsons from bothering me."

"You have wunderbaar elders here. Keep following their advice." By now, they were at the market.

Gracie looked all around her as she disembarked the buggy. Not seeing anyone or feeling their presence, she sighed in relief and started to pull containers out. "We'll just take everything in, and then set them out once it's all inside."

"What does your mamm normally do here?"

"She sells her baked items as well. Her containers are clear and mine are the blue ones. Whatever sells, we'll take the money to her and she can take it to the bank when she feels well again."

Walking back and forth, the two girls continued talking about the stalking situation. "What else are you doing?"

"First thing, I won't sing in public anymore. Just in case they're hanging around here. Second, if I see them, I ignore them and others intervene with them for me. That's at Deacon Bontrager's direction."

Molly shivered. "Are they here?"

"Nee. I don't feel like I'm being stared at today. And I hope it stays that way! For gut."

"I pray you are right." By now, both girls were busy opening the plastic containers and arranging the baked items on their booth tables. What didn't fit was kept inside the boxes and kept in reserve for the times when goods on the tables ran out. Shortly after, customers—Amish and Englisch—began to move through the now-open store, browsing the offerings.

Gracie felt comfortable, in her element as she interacted with her customers. During breaks when customers weren't around, Gracie had to force herself to remember not to sing, just in case. Tempted to hum under her breath, she sighed and castigated herself. While she was taking a short break with one of her friends, the other girl commented on the lack of songs.

CHAPTER 6

"I can't. I promised myself. And my parents, Abe and the deacon. That's what got me into this situation in the first place." Gracie sighed, feeling sad, as though something precious had been stolen from her.

"That's right. Well, are those people around?"

"I hope not. I don't feel like I'm being spied on. Before, when they were snooping around, I got a spooked feeling, as if someone was just watching me. Abe says he caught them spying on him when he was leaving our house. He stood up in his wagon and just looked around. Next thing he knew, he heard two sets of footsteps running away behind the tree line."

Her friend gasped. "Mei Gott! And you haven't felt anything since then?"

Gracie paused, thinking. "Ya, maybe, two weeks or so? But I still won't go anywhere by myself, just in case. Mamm…" Gracie remembered she shouldn't be talking about the steps they were taking. With a gasp, she paused. "Uh… We're taking precautions. I can't talk about them."

"Okay. I understand. If I see them, I'll let you know."

"Denki. I feel gut today. Even with Mamm sick at home today, I feel like there isn't anyone staring at me."

"And you'll sing your lungs out when you get home!"

Gracie laughed outright. "Ya, I will!"

The day at the market ended uneventfully. Driving back home with Molly, Gracie was happy. She hadn't felt like someone was spying on her even one time. Though she had forced herself multiple times not to hum, much less sing, she still felt good. Pulling into the yard and heading toward the barn, she saw her uncle's buggy. "Go ahead. I'll take care of the horses."

"Nee, let me help. Daed won't have it any other way." Brushing and feeding the horses, Molly chatted with Gracie. Next, both of them stacked containers high in their arms.

"We'll put them on the back porch and take them inside, then wash them. I'll see how Mamm is feeling."

And I'll go home with Daed." Molly hugged Gracie in the kitchen. Seeing her Aunt Abigail sitting, dressed, at the kitchen table, she smiled. "I hope you're feeling better!"

"Much, denki. Did you two do well today?"

In response, Molly took out a bank deposit bag and handed it to Abigail. "Very well. Everything sold."

❦

In the carpentry shop, Abe paused after cutting several long pieces of lumber for the hutch he was assigned to make. Shutting the saw off, he grabbed his thermos and poured out the remainder of his coffee. Taking a swig, he grimaced at the bitter taste. He couldn't get his mind off something that had been bothering him for a few days—he hadn't felt the stealthy, sneaky presence of the Wilsons. It was as though they had finally accepted Gracie's refusal to participate in their mupsich competition. "Nee, I can't believe they just accepted it. No way."

While Abe's words were quiet, they were loud enough that his daed, Ben, heard them.

"Who's 'they?' And what didn't they accept?" Ben's gray eyes bore a look of confusion.

"'They,' meaning Paul and Melody Wilson. The two people who have been bothering Gracie about taking part in that stupid competition. As if!"

"Have they stopped bothering her?"

"It seems so." Carefully, Abe moved the cut lengths of lumber to his worktable. "We haven't felt them spying on us. I want to find out soon if they bothered Gracie at the market today. I just can't believe that, as hard as they chased her, they, all of a sudden, decided that it wasn't worth hassling her so much. They're up to something."

"But you think they will be back, right?"

"Ya. You've heard her sing at services. She has a true blessing from Gott. But that blessing has turned on her. Now, she can't sing in public. She refuses to sing anywhere that isn't services or at home. Not even in her yard!"

Hearing this, Ben let out a huge, gusty sigh. He had always enjoyed hearing Gracie sing. "Son, if you believe they'll be back, then you'd better be on the lookout. Every day, wherever you go. I agree with you. You have a gut head on your shoulders. Whether they wait for a few days or a few months, they know they would achieve something huge if they get her to agree to compete. What's the name of the show? "

Abe shrugged. "I'm not too sure. Something like, *America's Biggest*, nee. Uh, *America's Most...* or *The Country's Most Talented*. Ya, that's it!"

Ben gave a broad grin. "Son, you and me are going to town. We're going to buy a few needed supplies. Then, we're going to that sports pub or a restaurant with a television and we're going to ask about that show. Then, when the deacon gets back, we're going to go and talk to him, you and me."

Abe's answering grin was huge. ""Ya, Daed! I like that idea! How are we going to find out about that show?"

"Just ask. We'll come up with a reason why before we do."

In response, Abe jumped into the air, thrusting one hand over his head. "And, do you think we can find out who's responsible for finding people to compete?"

Here, Ben shook his head. "Nee! They'll figure out why. All we can do is find out just what kind of show this is. And what kind of talent they are looking for. Please go tell Anna that we won't be eating lunch here today."

Before buying the items they needed, Ben and

Abe stopped at a newer restaurant in town. Inside, they requested to be seated in an area close to the television set, which was tuned to local news. When an advertisement for the upcoming season of, *The Country's Most Talented* came on, they watched closely. As they did, Ben beckoned their server over. "Excuse me, but I have a question about that show. What kinds of people does it attract?"

"This show's been pretty popular for going on ten years. All kinds of people compete. Those who can sing, perform magic tricks, gymnastic routines, dancing, acrobatic routines, ventriloquists. It's a pretty good show, actually. My kids enjoy it when it's on."

"What do people win?"

"One winner receives something like two hundred fifty thousand dollars. And a contract to perform, either in New York City or Las Vegas." The server shifted from foot to foot, impatient to take their orders. "Are you ready to order?"

"Ya, we are. I'll have coffee and the special of the day. Abe?"

"Coffee for me, and uh, the cheeseburger with onion rings…no, french fries, please."

"I'll get this in for you." The server hurried toward the kitchen.

"So, we know that it's not just singers who are signed to compete. I wonder if people who haven't been found by people like the Wilsons can compete." Ben began to watch the short video clip of the past season's show.

"Gut question. I don't know. All we can do is learn as much as we can. Abe, I just had an idea. Let's get as much work done as we can before Saturday. I'd like to go to the library here."

"To do what?" Abe was intrigued.

"Get one of the librarians to get on the internet for us to research everything about what talent people like the people pursuing Gracie do. As far as I'm concerned..." The server was setting their coffee mugs and two small carafes of coffee on the table. He also set two small bowls with individual servings of cream down. "Thank you!" Ben said. After he left, Ben continued to speak. "As far as I'm concerned, as much information as we can get, we'll be better able to help Gracie stay away from them."

"I like that. Ya, let's get as much done as we can. Give the others the day off, ya?"

"Nee. I'll tell the manager what we're going to do and let him keep things running that day. No need to keep them from earning what they need."

Once father and son had made their decision, they ate their lunches. Twice more, commercials advertising the upcoming season of the competition program came on. Abe paid special attention to the clips showing singers competing. "Those singers are right gut, Daed. But nowhere near what Gracie can do."

Ben sighed. "Ya, she is really gut. I can see why those two keep pursuing her."

"Especially if they were to earn a commission if she wins the entire competition."

After swallowing his coffee, Ben looked outside, squinting against the cold brightness outside. "That's a good consideration, Abe." He and Abe spoke quietly, then paid and left. After going home, they unloaded their purchases and finished the rest of the day's work.

On Friday night, Abe snuggled Gracie in his arms as they talked. "Daed and I are going to town tomorrow. We're going to visit the library and get one of the librarians to help us find out as much as we can about shows like the one you're trying to avoid. And how contestants get on the show."

Gracie, not wanting to leave the warmth of Abe's arms, turned slightly, looking at his calm, handsome face. "Really? Your daed agreed to do this?"

"It was his idea, actually. We went to town to buy

things we needed. We stopped at one of those restaurants with televisions and just watched the advertisements for the show." Abe sighed. "The singers are gut, but nowhere near how gut you are. While I don't want the Wilsons to come after you again, I can understand why they don't want to stop."

"About that, Abe. I haven't felt their presence here for a few days, maybe a week."

"Me, either. That means nothing. They haven't stopped. They're just lying low."

Gracie sighed. "That's what I think, too. They don't want to lose me. What they forget is they never got me—and they never will." Gracie's voice was determined and low. Her face bore a characteristic look of determination.

"You have the entire community helping you."

"Thank you! Because they will come back."

"Do you still watch what's going on when you go out?"

"Ya! Didn't you see me when we were going to the restaurant?"

"Ya, I did. And that's gut. Keep doing that. And let us know if you feel like you're being watched again. Or if they try to contact you in any way."

"I will." She shivered, remembering the spooky feeling of being watched. "I don't want to think about that. I just want to enjoy our time together."

The remainder of the evening, Abe and Gracie talked quietly about their upcoming plans. He suggested they go to the small diner near the entrance to their community. As she had told Abe she continued to do, Gracie was watchful of everyone that passed them on the road. She was also trying to stay alert for the feeling that she was being watched.

"Let's go in before your eyes fall out of your head." Abe teased Gracie gently.

Gracie giggled, feeling as though Abe understood her. Staying close to him, she hurried inside. She looked around by habit, praying she wouldn't see either one of the Wilsons.

Abe did the same thing, feeling complete relief when he didn't spot either one of the promoters.

"So, Abe, tell me more about this plan of yours for tomorrow." Holding her hot mug of tea within both hands, Gracie looked into Abe's gentle, gray eyes.

Abe shrugged. "It was Daed's idea. We're going to ask the librarian for as much information as possible about this kind of television show and how the contestants are brought in. This way, if the Wilsons come back, we'll be ready." Abe didn't want to worry Gracie with the knowledge that the Wilsons would come back.

Taking a bite of her peach pie, Gracie sighed. "That sounds like a great idea. I wish I could go with you. But Mamm just got well. So we'll spend tomorrow catching up on the cleaning."

"Well, since this Sunday isn't a meeting Sunday, I'll come over and tell you what we learn."

Gracie liked the idea and they enjoyed the rest of their date. She shivered as the cold air snuck in her coat and under the hem of her dress. Hunching over, she hugged her waist to warm up.

Abe, seeing Gracie huddling, wrapped an arm around her. "Better?"

"Ya. But we're going to have to be separate when we get back home. If someone sees us…"

"I know." Abe had been present when the elders had visited his oldest brother and parents. Someone had seen his brother fully embracing his girlfriend and took a report to the elders. The visit had made a vivid impression on Abe. As a result, he scrupulously obeyed the rules. As they approached the boundary of their community, he slowly removed his arm from Gracie's shoulders.

Gracie reluctantly moved away, wrapping her arms around her middle again. Less than five minutes later, one of the ministers rode past slowly.

"Minister Lee, how are you?" Abe smiled widely, both hands on the horses' reins.

"I'm gut, Abe. How about you? Gracie? How are you?"

Abe answered first. "Gut. Daed and I are going to town tomorrow. We want to get as much information from the library as we can about this show and even the talent people who keep harassing Gracie. We figure if we have this knowledge, it'll help Gracie to stay clear of them."

"Gut! I like that you're helping her out."

"Denki, Minister. I'm gut, too. Mamm was sick this week, so I was doing a lot of what she normally does. So, I'm a little tired."

"Well, it's cold and Gracie looks like she's feeling it. I'd better let you two go. I'm glad to hear of your efforts, Abe. Thank your daed for me."

"You're welcome. I will. G'night." Abe started moving forward again. As he did, he got the spooky feeling again. Stopping the buggy, he turned and hollered out to the minister. "Sir, can you come here?" Abe wheeled the buggy around. Coming even with the minister's buggy, he spoke quickly and quietly. "Sir, I just got a weird feeling. Like we're being watched. It's like the feeling we got before, when the Wilsons were chasing after Gracie."

The minister didn't visibly react. Instead, he hunched down slightly as if he were cold. Now that Abe had spoken, he got an eerie sense of someone watching them. "Take Gracie home, using a different route. I'll follow you, and then go to my destination using side roads."

Abe pulled ahead of the minister and started moving down the road faster than he would normally go. As he did so, he sensed that the Wilsons were, once again, hidden in the tree line, just watching them.

Gracie tried to shrink down so she was as invisible as possible. She had gotten the eerie sense at the same time as Abe. Feeling the fear and tension collecting in her back and between her shoulder blades, she forced herself to relax. "They aren't coming after you. Calm down. Breathe deeply."

As Gracie tried to regulate her breaths, Abe asked her what she was saying.

"Nothing really. Just telling myself not to jump out of this buggy and run screaming home."

"Nee, don't jump! Minister Lee is right behind us. You're safe." Turning again, Abe was on the road that ran just in back of the Troyer home. Pulling in through the rear fence, he stopped the horses just in front of the high porch. "Let's get inside." Abe turned his head, seeing the minister riding past. He slipped into the kitchen, closing the door securely behind him and Gracie.

Abigail came into the kitchen. "Gracie! Abe, what happened? Gracie, you look scared!"

"They're back, Mamm." Gracie gulped back a huge sob, not wanting to cry. I can't even enjoy a single evening out!"

"Sit down. Coffee? Tea?"

"Tea for me. Abe?" Gracie swiped a few stray tears from her cheeks.

"Coffee, please."

Jon came into the kitchen. "I just heard. What did you feel? Did you see anything?"

"We just felt like we were being watched. We saw Minister Lee as I was bringing Gracie home. He followed us after telling me to take a different route home. He just went to his own destination using a different route."

"Well, I'm wondering if it's worth going out there to look for them."

"Jon, nee! What if they have a weapon this time?" Abigail extended her hand toward her husband.

"Mister Troyer, this is what my daed and I are doing tomorrow. We're going to town and stopping at the library so we can get as much information as possible about these kinds of television shows and how the contestants get on the shows. We figure that the more information we have about these reality shows, the better we'll be able to help Gracie."

"Gracie? What do you think?" Jon looked at Gracie through lowered, bushy eyebrows.

"I like their idea, Daed. We don't know anything about these shows. Abe, why don't you tell Daed and Mamm how you got this idea?"

"We decided to go to town and stop in at one of the newer restaurants with televisions mounted on the walls. We also talked to one of the servers who was able to give us a little information about how the contestants get on the shows. This was after he suggested we go to the library tomorrow."

Jon nodded, thinking. "It is a wunderbaar idea. Please come back and tell us what you learn. I suppose you'll be getting this information from the internet, ya?"

"Ya. We'll ask one of the reference librarians to help us out." Abe finished his coffee and motioning with his head, indicated he was going to stand out on the porch. "If I don't get the feeling we're being stared at, I'll go home. Daed wanted me to be home early." Stepping outside, he looked around, peering into the trees. Turning, he waved to the Troyers. "I don't get the feeling they're out here. I'd better go. Gracie, I'll be seeing you tomorrow. Hopefully, with lots of information."

"Denki! See you tomorrow!"

While Abe didn't feel like he was being stared at as he got into his buggy, he got an overwhelming sense as he was taking side roads home. Whispering a special code word to his horses, he told them to pick up their speed. "Trixie, Dollie, move!" In response, the horses began to canter. Abe was home a little more quickly than normal. Hurrying the horses into the barn, he unhitched them and got them ready for the night. Making sure both doors on the barn were securely locked, he shot out from the back door and ran into the house through the kitchen. Trying not to slam the door, he leaned against it, closing his eyes and trying to slow his hammering heart.

"Abe! What's wrong?"

"They're out there again. Gracie had one blessed week of peace, and now they're back. And she's scared out of her mind."

"It's gut, then, that we're going to the library tomorrow. Did you tell her about that?"

"Her and her parents. I ran into their house with her when I got her home. We stayed long enough for a cup of coffee and to talk about what we're doing. Mister and Missus Troyer both liked it."

"Excellent! And now, we can't do anything about those two crazy people outside. So, I suggest we get to bed. We have a long day ahead of us tomorrow."

"Goodnight, then." Upstairs in his room, Abe paced back and forth, trying to burn off the frustration and fear he was feeling. Peering out his window, he tried to see if he could spot anyone outside. He was about to give up and go to bed when he thought he saw the tiniest glint. Squinting, he focused on the spot. *Ya, I do see something! Jewelry, maybe? A metal clasp on a woman's purse?* Grateful that he hadn't lit his lamp, Abe continued to look at the spot. Soon, the microscopic glint began to bob and move away from its spot. Abe found that now that his eyes were getting used to the deep blackness outside, he was able to see the outlines of two people—a man and woman. Resting some of his weight on his hands, which were lying on the windowsill, he saw that he could now pick out a short coat on the woman. The man wore a jacket. Because of how dark it was, he couldn't tell the colors of their clothing. Next, as Abe's shoulders and neck tightened, becoming extremely tense, he saw them stopping at a car parked close to the end of the lane. *They know where I live now! Abe, don't be mupsich. They probably know where the elders live!* Hearing the muffled sound of the car engine, Abe sighed with relief. *Hopefully, they won't be back tonight.* He promised himself that he would tell his daed what he saw in the morning.

The next morning, Abe clattered downstairs, yawning. He hadn't been able to get to sleep right away. Instead, he had mentally ridden along with the Wilsons as they sped back to Philadelphia. He had wanted to be a fly on the window of their car, listening to their conversation.

"Abe, did you sleep well?" Martha, the house-keeper and cook, turned, looking at Abe with concern in her eyes.

"Nee, Martha. That couple that's been bothering Gracie came back last night. We realized they were just watching us as I took her home. They followed me home as well."

Ben walked into the kitchen. "Abe, you look terrible. You're going to bed early tonight."

Abe didn't say anything. He knew he could nap in the buggy coming and going. Instead, he told his daed what he'd seen outside his bedroom window. "I saw the glint of metal, probably a woman's purse or jewelry, then I saw their bodies. They walked back to their car, which was parked near the end of our lane."

"They know where we live. On our way to the library, we're talking to one of the elders. They're going to confront her again. Sooner rather than later."

❦

Tue to his plan, Abe catnapped on the way to the library. Minister Summy had advised them to bring back as much information as the librarians could find on the internet. "I don't have to tell you to be on the lookout for those two. Deacon Bontrager should be back later this afternoon. I'll tell him what you told me. I think it's high time for a meeting at his place."

"We'll take the information we find to this meeting. Should Gracie and her parents be there?"

"It would help. I'll leave written messages for everyone. Time and place, most likely tomorrow."

"Gut. We'd better go. We want to get there when the library opens." As it turned out, Abe and his daed were nearly an hour early. "Man, Daed! They start their workday when our mornings are half gone! Look!" Abe gestured to the daily opening schedule posted on the front window of the library.

"Coffee while we wait?"

"Ya. With donuts." Abe grinned. He still felt the fuzzy edges of sleep tugging at him. The coffee would help.

After wolfing down a double serving of donuts

and three cups of coffee each, Abe and Ben went back to the library, which was just about to open.

"Yes, we need a librarian to help us. We can't use the internet, so we need someone who can get the information we need for us." Ben explained quietly what he and Abe needed.

"Certainly." The reference librarian, a no-nonsense woman with salt-and-pepper hair cut in an attractive short style, turned and beckoned to a younger woman. "Melissa, these two gentlemen need your help. They can't use the internet, so they need you to do the searches based on what they say they need."

Melissa smiled at her supervisor. "Thanks, Becky. Sir? If you and your son would come over here, we can use one of the smaller computer rooms."

"Miss, thank you for helping us."

"You're welcome. What is it you need?"

"As you can tell, we're Amish. We can't do some things that are a huge part of your life. Like using the computer or the internet. Competing in talent shows. Allowing our pictures to be taken, showing our faces. Being on television. My son here, Abe, has a friend at home. She has a voice that is Gott's own gift. Well, recently, she was finishing a day of work at the Amish market. She was putting her bakery containers away, along with her day's earnings. As she did so, she was singing, as was her habit.

"A non-Amish couple came in and asked her to sing another hymn. When she finished, they told her that they had to sign her up for the televised talent competition they are representing—"

"Wait… *The Country's Most Talented*?" Melissa had a smile on her face.

"Exactly. She told them she couldn't take part because of our community's rules. And she doesn't want to take part in this show. They haven't listened. They keep showing up and bothering her. No matter what she tells them. So, because we prefer not to reach out to law enforcement, we figured we'd best educate ourselves about these talent competitions, educate Gracie, the young woman we're talking about and just figure out a way to keep them from bothering her anymore."

"Okay, before we start, is she aware of what you're doing? Does she approve?" Melissa wore a look of concern.

"Yes, to both. She loved the idea when Abe told her. Abe, will you tell Melissa what happened to the two of you last night?"

Abe recounted the now-familiar feeling of being spied on and his helter-skelter ride home.

"Wow! It's a wonder you didn't overturn your

buggy. Let's get started, then. I'm guessing you want to learn about what these shows are. And how contestants get signed up with them?"

"Ya, exactly. And anything else you can find out. Like, do talent scouters, or whatever, help the show's owners or whoever to find talented people who have a chance of winning?"

Melissa rubbed her finger under her lower lip, thinking. Coming up with several ideas, she jotted them down and turned the sheet of her notes toward Ben and Abe. "Is that what you're looking for?"

Abe read strings of unconnected words. "How do you find what we need with words that don't seem connected to each other?"

"The internet will respond by giving us search results—tens of thousands of them—that will have some of the information you need. We may need to print out information from several sources to get everything you need."

"Daed? Go ahead?"

Ben nodded. "Let's get started."

An hour and a half later, Melissa removed a thick stack of pages from the printer. Arranging them so they would read logically, she stapled them together for Abe, handing them to him. "You'll get an idea of the topic of each set of notes from the headline. Not every talent competition does everything the same. I included as much as I could find about the show that's interested in your friend so you can develop responses to their overtures. Mister Lapp, I strongly urge you to contact law enforcement if these people don't stop bothering your son's friend. That's harassment and they can get into legal trouble doing that."

"We're probably going to let them think that. They don't know very much about our traditions, practices and beliefs, if anything. So I doubt they know we don't like to get law enforcement involved."

Melissa's face was doubtful. "Well...if you think that'll work. But if they don't stop, or if they start to escalate their overtures toward her, I worry about her safety and yours."

Abe and Ben looked at each other. Abe was shaken and he began to tense up, feeling the pressure in his neck.

"We'll talk to our elders. It'll be up to them." Ben said these soft-spoken words more as a way to soothe Melissa. "Abe, we'd better get home to see how the carpenters did with today's work. Melissa, thank you." Ben extended his hand toward Melissa, who shook it.

"You're welcome. If you have any more questions, come in and ask us. One of us will be willing to help you out."

In the buggy, Abe went through the printouts, reading out interesting or pertinent sections to Ben. "We need to go through these in detail once the men have gone home."

⚜

After sending the men home and cleaning the shop, Abe and Ben sat at the kitchen table, discussing everything they read. Abe sat back stretching his arms over his head. "Daed, Melissa was very helpful today." He turned at a knock on the door. "I'll get it."

Opening the door, he saw Deacon Bontrager on the porch. "Deacon! You're back! Come in!" Abe opened the door wide.

The deacon walked in, smiling.

Ben jumped up and poured a cup of coffee for the elder. "Come and sit with us. We were just talking about everything that's happened in my absence. And it seemed more happened last night?"

"Ya." Abe told the deacon what he and Gracie had sensed and what he had seen from his bedroom window the night before. "And today, Daed and I went to the library. The reference librarian found all of this for us, about talent competitions, how they are operated, and how the talent was found and signed.

The librarian tried pretty hard to urge us to call law enforcement."

"Nee. Only if things get really bad. May I read what this librarian found for you?" Sipping his coffee, Eli went through the materials, page by page. "Well! She was *very* helpful. This gives us a lot more to work on. Now, I understand someone had the idea of implying to the Wilsons that, if they don't leave Gracie or anyone else alone, we will seek legal help. As far as that goes, I would rather give them the *impression* that we're going to do that. Then see if they stop. It seems that if they value their jobs with this company, they will cease all their efforts."

Abe and Ben looked at each other soberly. "Ya, if we can just give them the idea that we're willing to involve law enforcement. I don't want to be the first to call the police." Abe was beginning to feel overwhelmed. As a result, he was rapidly developing a stress headache. Jumping up, he grabbed the bottle of ibuprofen he knew his daed kept in the drawer of the hutch.

"Ya, I think that's an excellent idea. Abe, try some more coffee. That may help your headache." The deacon looked up, seeing Abe massaging the base of his neck. "This information is wunderbaar. Now, I understand we're having a meeting at my place tomorrow. Can I take this and make copies for everyone?"

Ben looked at the wall clock. "If you get to town quickly, you may be able to get into the library."

Eli looked at the clock. "Ya, I'd better get. Mary won't be happy if I'm late to supper." Clapping his black hat on his head, he let himself out the door.

"Daed, I'm going to take a nap. I'm going out with Gracie tonight and I want to get rid of this headache."

"Go nap. I want to think anyway." Ben sat at the table, reading random packets of information from the second set Melissa had printed, trying to put everything in order in his mind. As he did so, he rearranged the packets, jotting little notes on the top pages.

❧

When Abe woke, he felt much better, his headache completely gone. He dressed quickly and ran a comb through his hair. "I need a haircut before long." Downstairs, he saw Ben finishing the supper their housekeeper had made. "Daed, I'm leaving to pick Gracie up. I'll be home later on."

"Be careful, son." Ben looked up from one of the sheaves of paper he was studying.

Arriving at the movie theater, Abe and Gracie bought snacks and went into the theater for the movie they wanted to see. They were easy to spot, as they were wearing their usual Plain clothing. Gracie's white prayer cap was easy to spot in the dim theater. As they watched the movie and munched their popcorn, they weren't aware that Paul and Melody Wilson had come in to see the same movie.

Paul carefully nudged Melody, who had their large sodas in her hands. "Hey! Look down there, close to the middle of that row down there. Recognize them?"

Melody, who had opted to wear her contacts, easily spotted Gracie. Next to her, she saw Gracie's tall and muscled boyfriend. "Gracie! But she has that guy with her."

"Watch and see if she leaves the theater for more snacks or to use the women's room. If she does, you go and catch up to her. She probably won't make a scene."

"Sweet! That may work…if she feels the call of nature." Melody sat next to her husband and they settled in to watch the comedy being screened. However, they weren't able to pay full attention to the action on-screen—both of them kept flicking their glances over to Gracie. Melody, using her cell phone, quickly and surreptitiously checked the time that had passed. Seeing that the movie would be ending in less than thirty minutes, she began to feel panic rising. "Paul! The movie's nearly over! And she hasn't left for the restroom or anything!"

"All we can do is try to catch them before they can leave."

But circumstances were against them. Abe had quickly turned around after feeling as if they were under close observation. He had leaned over, putting his mouth close to Gracie's ear. He'd told her that the Wilsons were in the theater. "Nee! Don't turn around! We'll leave as soon as it ends." Abe, not moving his head, allowed his eyes to sweep the rows of seats. "There's so many people in here that I think we can get away before they can reach us."

Gracie sighed. "Okay. I wish they would just leave us alone!" Knowing that Abe would do everything he could to protect the two of them, she forced herself to relax and focus on the movie.

"Okay, the credits are going to roll. We're going to wait until we see people getting up to leave, then we'll blend in w…uh, just get out of here. There's no blending in with what we're wearing." Abe gauged the numbers of people passing them, some looking with curiosity at them. "Okay. Now!"

Gracie got up and, gripping Abe's hand, followed, walking quickly. Soon, they were caught up in a scrum of people. As the doors neared, she held her breath, praying that the people around them would be protection enough. Holding her breath, she counted down the seconds until they could get outside and into Abe's buggy.

"Gracie! Gracie!"

"Don't turn your head. Just follow me!" Abe broke into a trot, hoping Gracie could keep up with him.

Gracie relied on her ability to enter into a ground-eating stride. She kept up easily with Abe.

Abe pushed on the door handle, swinging it wide as he and Gracie broke into a fast run. As they neared his buggy, he swept Gracie up in his arms, settling her easily on the seat. Vaulting up, he landed and grabbed the reins simultaneously. "Shaaaa! Go, now!" The horses, startled at Abe's shout, bounded forward. Quickly Abe got them out of town. "Look back. Are they following us?"

Gracie squinted against the cold night air. Looking behind them, she didn't see any lights from a small car. "I don't see them."

"Thank Gott. Okay, I'm going to get you home and probably wait at your house until we know they won't come to Crawford County or your place." Abe held back on telling her that they had followed him to his own house.

Once in the Troyer home, they told Jon and Abigail what had happened. "He got us out of there as fast as he could, Daed."

"Abe, I am so grateful to you for protecting Gracie. But maybe from now on, you should get together within the confines of our community."

"Daed! We haven't done anything wrong!" Gracie's voice bore a note of disappointment as she reacted to Jon's decision.

"Daughter! It's our job to make sure you're safe! These people aren't going to leave you alone if you and your friends go into town! That's it. Go to bed, and I want you to think of the fourth commandment. Go! Now!" Jon wasn't afraid to lay the law down on his children.

Gracie, knowing she'd crossed the line, pressed her full lips together, not willing to risk what she would say if she had dared to say anything more. Rising from the kitchen table, she waved quickly at Abe, and then hurried upstairs. Once in her room, she ripped her prayer cap from her head. "Maybe I should just not be baptized. Maybe I should just give in to what the Wilsons want. Compete in this mupsich show. If I'm really as gut as they claim, maybe I can win that money and give it to Mamm and Daed."

Unpinning her dress, Gracie lapsed into fantasies of wearing clothing with buttons and zippers, as opposed to straight pins. She fantasized about competing and finding out that the country had picked her for her voice. Soon, she realized what she was doing. Shaking her head hard, she sent her long hair swirling and flying around her torso and face. *Nee, Gracie! Dad sent you upstairs early because you back-talked him! Now, put your gown on, get ready for bed and read those Bible verses on obedience.*

Feeling ashamed and embarrassed, Gracie dressed quickly in her gown. Flipping her hair over one shoulder, she expertly and quickly braided it so it wouldn't tangle as badly. In bed, she made sure she had plenty of oil in her lamp, and then began to read the Bible. *Honor your father and your mother, so you will have a long life in the land the Lord has given you.* Next, she looked for and studied other Bible verses on obedience to parents. Finding one of her favorite, she went to the Book of Ephesians and went to Chapter six, verse one. *Children, obey your parents as the Lord says, because he is right.* Reading further, she came to a part she had never paid attention to before. *Fathers, do not exasperate your children; instead, bring them up in the training of the Lord.*

She found several other Bible verses, and seeing that they all had the same basic message, she realized how she had very nearly brought dishonor on her parents. *I can't go and compete because it will bring shame to Mamm, Daed and our whole family.* I can be mad at them, ya, but I need to listen to them and do what they say. I can't argue with them, either. Feeling a strong wave of sleepiness, Gracie yawned. Setting her Bible on the small wood table, she rolled over, and then remembered the lamp. Rising, she blew it out. *Abe!* Moving quietly to the window, she saw that his wagon and horses were gone. *What time is it?* Yawning once again, she gave up trying to figure that out. Rolling so she faced the window, she fell asleep almost immediately.

Waking as she saw the first delicate tendrils of sunlight tiptoeing into her room, Gracie stretched. Feeling the cold air, she grimaced. Next, she threw her covers back and slipped her feet into slippers. Hurrying to the bathroom, she brushed her teeth and did her business. Combing her waist-length hair, she put it into a ponytail, and then rolled it into a large bun. In her room, she dressed. Her gaze falling on her Bible, she remembered the past evening's discipline. *I need to apologize to both Mamm and Daed.* Downstairs, she began working on the biscuits and laid several slices of bacon into the large frying pan.

"Gut morning, daughter. Are you feeling better today?" Abigail was soft-spoken, but she wore an expression that told Gracie what she needed to do.

"Ya, Mamm. I am so sorry. I had no excuse for talking back to you and Daed last night."

"Ya. That's right. And Daed only made that decision because he's trying to protect you from people who want to use you. Ya, daughter, you have a beautiful voice, but Gott does not want you to use it in a competition."

"I understand." Gracie's voice was soft and quiet.

Stomping his feet on the mat outside, Jon came into the house.

"Daed, I am so sorry for what I said to you last night. I had no excuse for doing so. I know you're just trying to make sure that I'm safe."

"I am right happy to hear that, Gracie. Did you read those Bible readings last night?"

"Ya, I did. I think you and Mamm were already asleep by the time I blew my lamp out. Abe's buggy was gone, anyway, when I looked out my window. Daed, what does it mean when Gott told fathers not to exasperate their children? I couldn't figure that part out."

CHAPTER 7

"Simply that, in our efforts to protect our children, we are to teach them Gott's way and let Him do His work. And let them know that whenever they need His help and protection, He will be there."

"So...do I still need to get together with my friends only within our community?"

"Ya. I'm sorry, daughter. It may feel like you're the one being punished. But we are simply trying to keep these people from getting to you."

"Ya. I don't like it. But I do understand. Also, if I were to do this show, it would bring shame on you and Mamm."

"Not to mention the community."

"Daed, please help me. If they get to me and I can't get away, what am I supposed to do or say?" As

Gracie asked her question, she noticed that it was snowing outside. "How long has it been snowing?"

"For less than thirty minutes. It's not going to get serious until this afternoon, sometime. This comes from the television news, which Eli saw when he was on his way home yesterday. We're all going to that meeting. Including you. Deacon Bontrager spoke to a bishop in an adjoining community. And he learned a lot. We'll talk about that over at his house. Once we finish breakfast, we'll go."

❦

A t the deacon's house, everyone sat around the kitchen table. The deacon's wife served coffee, tea and cinnamon coffee cake.

"Okay, this is what I found out." The deacon launched into a long description of what he and the bishop had discussed. "He doesn't want us to rely on law enforcement. He did say that if we need to, we can ask librarians to get onto the internet and find information that we need. Which Abe and Ben did, yesterday. And they found out quite a bit.

"As it turns out, people generally audition for these 'reality show competitions.' They are not scripted. But they do rely on a certain element of drama to keep people watching week after week. So, in a way, they require contestants to become competitors. And the camera operators capture all the dramatic moments. Those moments are more often than not shared with the viewing audience.

"So, Gracie, you need some support. That is clear. This is what we are going to do. I understand from your daed that you can't leave the community until this is resolved, ya?"

"Ya. Deacon, I don't like it, but I will comply. What else can I do? Because they come here. They hide themselves and they spy on me. They have spied on me when I've been with Abe!"

"How did you realize that?" Deacon Eli leaned forward, waiting for Gracie's or Abe's answer.

Gracie let out a shivery sigh. "We were coming home from an evening out with our friends. I felt like someone was just...*staring* at me, and not stopping. Abe got me home as fast as he could but..."

"But what?"

"They stayed around. A few days later, he told me he got that same creepy sensation. He made them leave when he stopped his buggy and stood up to look all around. And they've done that a few more times."

"What happened last night?"

"We went to the comedy movie showing at the theater. Abe spotted them partway through the movie and, just after it ended, he told me they were in there. We got away from them, but Deacon, I am getting so sick of them bothering me!" Gracie felt unwanted tears beginning to fall down her cheeks. Grasping the napkin that was placed into her hand, she sighed and wiped at her cheeks.

"Okay. You stay here in Crawford County when you are with your friends. And, if we see them here, looking for you, then we will stop them from looking for you. Oh. And one last thing. Maybe you shouldn't be selling your goods at the market. They found you there, so they're likely to continue looking for you in public areas."

"What about selling my baked goods?"

"Gracie, I will do so." Ann Bontrager, the deacon's wife stepped forward. "I am happy to give my time so you can be protected. And once we've managed to convince these people to leave you alone, you can resume your normal activities."

Gracie began to cry in earnest. After a few minutes of silent weeping, she exhaled and inhaled a long breath, gaining control of herself again. "Denki, Missus Bontrager. I am so grateful to you!"

Two days later, Minister Summy came to the deacon's house with a disturbing report. "Deacon, those people chasing Gracie Troyer? I overheard them talking and they aren't giving up. The husband said he was 'in it for the long haul,' whatever that means. We need to go talk to the family and let them know this."

"Okay, let's go to pick up Thomas. We'll pick him up on the way to the Troyer's so we can talk to all of them together."

Both elders stopped at Thomas Lee's house, waiting until his wife brought him back from the barn.

"Ya, deacon, what is it? Dan, this must be serious." Thomas Lee was the second minister and third elder in the Crawford County community.

"Thomas, Dan overheard those two Englischers talking between themselves. They were taking about not giving up on getting Gracie Troyer into that program. I believe we need to go and warn the Troyers so they know." Deacon Eli shook his head sadly.

"We should also let Ben and Anna Lapp know as well. I heard tell they know that Abe and Gracie spend a lot of time together."

The deacon sighed. "Maybe we should discuss

this in services this Sunday."

Both ministers nodded, giving the deacon's words some thought. Minister Summy spoke. "We have to. We don't want to see this couple forcing Gracie to do something she doesn't want to do."

"Nee, Dan, I don't think it'll come to that. My main focus in discussing this in meeting is so the whole community knows what is happening. Some of the younger teens are questioning why Gracie even refused to compete."

Thomas grunted. While he was married, he still nursed a secret, tender regard for Gracie. He suspected she was seeing Abe Lapp and had long since reconciled himself to reality. Instead, he tried to keep an eye out for the girl, from a distance. "Ya. You're right, Deacon. Should we go?"

Abigail, hearing the knocking at the front door, answered it. "Deacon! Ministers! Is everything okay? Please, come in. Coffee?"

"Nee, Abigail, Everything isn't okay. We need to speak to your mann and to Gracie, if they are available. And ya, the coffee would be very welcome on this bitter day."

The men followed Abigail and sat, waiting.

"Gracie, go to the workshop and bring your daed inside, please."

Gracie, not knowing what was happening, hurried to obey. "Daed." She was breathless after running so fast to obey. "The elders are here and they say something is wrong!"

Jon gave his workers instructions and hurried alongside Gracie. "Deacon, ministers, what's wrong?"

"Coffee, Jon?" Abigail held the coffeepot in her hand.

"Ya, denki." Accepting his cup with a quiet 'thank you,' Jon listened to the elders.

"Jon, you might want to have your daughter and wife sit with us. It involves Gracie." The deacon spoke up first.

Gracie drew her breath in quickly. "It's them, isn't it?" She had to pull a chair out quickly—her legs wouldn't hold her up.

"Ya, Gracie, I am so sorry. Minister Summy, why don't you tell them what you told us?" The deacon leaned forward, feeling badly for Gracie.

Dan exhaled. "Gracie, I'm so sorry to be the one to tell you this. I was walking on the road leaving the community. I overheard a man and a woman talking about not giving up. At first, I didn't know what they were taking about. When they talked about 'her singing voice,' I realized who it was and who they were talking about. Are you still sure you don't want to take part in that show?"

"Ya! I don't want to. No matter that I can't. I just want them to leave me alone." Putting her hand over her mouth, she quelled the tears that wanted to fall. She refused to look up, not wanting anyone to see her tears.

"Gracie? Daughter, look at me." Jon issued a soft-voiced command. Waiting until Gracie raised her eyes, he continued. "Daughter, you're doing every-thing that you're supposed to be doing. Don't worry —you aren't in the wrong. It's them, these Englisch-ers, who are. We're going to discuss ways of keeping you safe so the Wilsons won't have an opportunity to get to you."

"Okay. Deacon? Is there any way we can get this over with really fast? Because I'm really ready for it to be over!"

"We will do our best, Gracie. But we are going to have to come up with a plan so we can protect you *and* have this nonsense come to an end. Jon, Abigail and you, Gracie, we are going to bring this up in meeting on Sunday. After the service has ended. Because we are going to have to set up with several men and teen boys to create a barrier between you, your parents and home so they can't get to you. The elders and I will come up with something and discuss it with you when we have something we believe will work. When we decide that something will work, hopefully before meeting on Sunday, we will request volunteers so you aren't alone—ever—until this ends. The only times you'll be alone are in your room at night. We hope to get the teen boys, both those who are in rumspringa and those who are awaiting that time, to help us out."

"Deacon, because of work, we'll have to schedule carefully." Jon brought up this reminder.

"Ya, we will. Denki, Jon. Gracie, are you still selling your baked items at market?"

"Nee. Your wife told me she will take over the selling until this ends. Please let her know that I am very grateful for her generous support." Gracie let out a long, sibilant sigh of gratitude and relief. She felt, strangely, a sense of support, even though she was still being tracked, if not harassed, by the Wilsons.

At meeting, the three ministers waited for the well of chattering and laughter to end. Looking from one side of the room to the other. Slowly, attendees at the service grew quiet, their eyes focused at the front of the room.

"Denki. If we can begin..." The three-hour ceremony started with the familiar hymns from the *Ausbund*. As she began to sing, Gracie reflexively looked around at the windows and doors, thinking of Melody and Paul Wilson. Not seeing any shadows, she let her full voice ring out. Her eyes closed as she remembered and sang the familiar, German words. Soon, her spirit was engulfed in Gott's love and gentle embrace. Next, the teachings began.

Finally, the sermons began. Everyone settled down, knowing it would be quite a while until they could stand up and move around. At the end of the series of teachings and sermons, people moved, some feeling stiff.

Gracie and Abigail moved together to the kitchen, stopping only when the deacon got their attention once more.

"You don't have to sit back down. I just want to let you know that one of our ministers overheard the couple that's been harassing Miss Troyer lately. He came to me and we pulled the other minister in to discuss what he overheard. Now, for those of you who don't know, Miss Troyer bakes for her living. But, because of these two people, she can't risk being at the market on sale days. Instead, my wife came forward and offered to help her out.

"The ministers and I went to the homes of several community members. We have asked the men and the teen boys to help in setting up a barrier between these Englischers and Miss Troyer, her parents and home. She is already doing everything we have requested of her. She isn't going outside our community boundaries. She's baking, but not selling, her goods. When she goes out on her errands, she goes with her mamm or one of her friends or close-by sisters. So, she is doing everything she can to stay away from these people. But she needs help. We are asking all adult and teen males to volunteer to help create a physical barrier. Boys who are still scholars cannot volunteer—Miss Stolzfus would object too greatly for that. We want boys 15 and up, as well as adult males. Deacon Lee is passing around a few pages of paper with days and times written down. Put your names down on the days and times when you can help out. We don't want to take you away from your own work, so volunteer only when you know you aren't committed to a work activity."

The gathering slowly moved into other areas of the large house. Children, now freed from the mandatory stillness, ran and screamed as they played with each other. The men rearranged the benches, setting long tables in between them. The women and girls began to bring food and beverages into the room, setting the beverages on a table at the front of the room.

In age groups, community members sat to eat. As each group finished eating, a different group took its place.

In the kitchen, Gracie worked quietly, not wanting to talk about her situation. She sighed, asking for patience, as a particularly snoopy and curious girl tried to get the details.

"Gracie, that is so horrible what you're going through! I can't *even* imagine." The girl covered her heart with one hand and sighed dramatically. "Please let me know if you need any help. Now, what happened?"

If Gracie hadn't been so worried, she would have been tempted to giggle. "Emily, I can't talk about it. I've promised the elders...unless you want to get in trouble with *them!*" Gracie turned Emily's dramatics back on the other girl, putting one hand on her heart and tipping her head as Emily had done.

Emily gasped. "Nee! No way!" She scuttled away as fast as she could move, not wanting to be seen by any of the ministers.

Gracie turned her lips inward and tried hard to hold giggles back. *That wasn't very nice. But I don't want to make my situation even worse.* She jumped as she felt her mother's hand land on her shoulder.

"Daughter, what was all of that with Emily about? And then that quirky little smile?"

"I'm sorry, Mamm. I had to smile. She was 'giving me support' for what I'm going through with the Wilsons." Gracie's voice was quiet as she spoke. "Then, as soon as she gave me that, she jumped straight into digging for the facts. I'm about to blow up with all of this. So I told her that I promised the elders I would stay quiet about everything. Then I told her I would tell her —if she didn't mind getting in trouble with *them.* She left right away." Now, Gracie stifled a true laugh.

Trying not to laugh herself, Abigail put her fingers over her mouth. "You'd just better be careful. I'm glad you told her that you can't say anything. That's a wunderbaar idea, anyway."

"Denki, Mamm. It just feels…well, wrong, if I say anything. At least until this mess is all over."

Gracie and Abigail heard a scuffle and raised voices at the front door where services and the meeting were taking place. Moving to the entryway to the kitchen, Gracie gasped. "Mamm! It's the Wilsons!"

"Get back into the pantry. Close the door and don't come out until I say they are gone." Abigail hurried to the front door. "Deacon, why are they here? How did they find out where today's service was to take place?"

Eli raised his eyes to the ceiling of the living room. Sighing heavily, he spoke. "They saw all the buggies and came to the natural conclusion that if other community members are here, Gracie would be here. Is she well away from them?"

"Ya." Turning to face the Wilsons, Abigail's face transformed into a mask of pure anger. "And she isn't coming out until I tell her that it's safe to do so." Her voice developed a hardness that was rarely evident.

"But...I...we only wanted to talk to her! Just to see if there's any way she can compete without violating any rules or whatever..."

Deacon Eli sighed, feeling his patience rapidly disappearing. "Mister and Missus Wilson, we have told you many times that she cannot compete. There is the matter of her face being broadcast on televisions or whatever it's called. Then, we here don't believe in or allow competition. Third, she would be running the risk of becoming full of pride, which is a real sin. So, nee, she won't be coming out and she won't be talking to you. You are running a real risk by constantly trying to get in contact with her. Go. Now!" The deacon's voice bore a subtle growl, something that happened when he was angered.

"Please? She would have a real shot at winning the—"

"Missus Wilson, we don't care. She doesn't care about winning money. She has something here that is much more valuable. She has already told you, more than once that she isn't going to agree to compete. Do you finally understand?" Jon was absolutely fed up. Looking in back of him, he saw rooms full of picnic tables and people who were waiting to be served their lunch. "Now, if you don't mind, your presence here is delaying lunch. Why don't you understand the clues we are giving you and just go?"

Closed into the pantry, Gracie closed her eyes and tried to listen to what was being said. It wasn't too hard. Everyone who was waiting to eat had fallen quiet, making it easier to hear the voices in the living room. "Oh, please just leave! I don't want to talk... Wait. They need to hear it from me. Mamm, I'm sorry. I have to tell them." Opening the door, she rushed into the living room. Confronting the Wilsons, she spoke. "There is nothing you could say or offer to me that would induce me to change my mind. Now go!"

The End.

THANK YOU FOR READING!

I hope you enjoyed reading this book as I loved writing it! If so, grab the next book in the series here **OR you can save big and GET ALL 3 BOOKS in one boxed set here.** There is a sample of the next book in the series in the next chapter.

Lastly, **if you enjoyed this book and want to continue to support my writing, please leave this book a review** to let everyone know what you thought of the series. It's the best thing you can do to keep indie authors like me writing. (And if you find something in the book that – YIKES – makes you think it deserves less than 5-stars, drop me a line at Rachel.stoltzfus@globagrafxpress.com, and I'll fix it if I can.)

All the best,
Rachel

AMISH STAR – BOOK 2

She's ready to leave the nest...but can she put her family, and love, behind her?

Gracie's voice is a gift from Gott, and she loves to sing. But as she steps into the spotlight, the strictures of her community's Ordnung become too much, and Gracie decides to leave. The two Englischers who discovered her talent agree to sponsor and mentor her in her new career, and Gracie wants to be happy, but is a life of fame and fortune really what she wants?

And can she truly leave her love, Daniel Byler, behind?

Find out in Amish Star – Book 2, the second book of the This Little Amish Light series. Amish Star –

Book 2 is an uplifting, Christian romance about the power of faith and the gifts we all share.

PROLOGUE

Gracie and Abigail heard a scuffle and raised voices at the front door where services and the meeting were taking place. Moving to the entryway to the kitchen, Gracie gasped. "Mamm! It's the Wilsons!"

"Get back into the pantry. Close the door and don't come out until I say they are gone." Abigail hurried to the front door. "Deacon, why are they here? How did they find out where today's service was to take place?"

Eli raised his eyes to the ceiling of the living room. Sighing heavily, he spoke. "They saw all the buggies and came to the natural conclusion that, if other community members are here, Gracie would be here. Is she well away from them?"

"Ya." Turning to face the Wilsons, Abigail's face

transformed into a mask of pure anger. "And she isn't coming out until I tell her that it's safe to do so." Her voice developed a hardness that was rarely evident.

"But...I...we only wanted to talk to her! Just to see if there's any way she can compete without violating any rules or whatever..."

Deacon Eli sighed, feeling his patience rapidly disappearing. "Mister and Missus Wilson, we have told you many times that she cannot compete. There is the matter of her face being broadcast on televisions or whatever it's called. Then, we here don't believe in or allow competition. Third, she would be running the risk of becoming full of pride, which is a real sin. So...nee, she won't be coming out and she won't be talking to you. You are running a real risk by constantly trying to get in contact with her. Go. Now!" The deacon's voice bore a subtle growl, something that happened when he was angered.

"Please? She would have a real shot at winning the—"

"Missus Wilson, we don't care...she doesn't care about winning money. She has something here that is much more valuable. She has already told you, more than once that she isn't going to agree to compete. Do you finally understand?" Jon was absolutely fed up. Looking in back of him, he saw rooms full of picnic tables and people who were waiting to be served their lunch. "Now, if you don't mind, your presence here is delaying lunch. Why don't you understand the clues we are giving you and just go?"

Closed into the pantry, Gracie closed her eyes and tried to listen to what was being said. It wasn't too hard. Everyone who was waiting to eat had fallen quiet, making it easier to hear the voices in the living room. "Oh, please just leave! I don't want to talk... Wait. They need to hear it from me. Mamm, I'm sorry. I have to tell them." Opening the door, she rushed into the living room. Confronting the Wilsons, she spoke. "There is nothing you could say or offer to me that would induce me to change my mind. Now go!"

THANK YOU FOR READING!

I hope you enjoyed reading this book as I loved writing it! If so, **grab the next book in the series here OR you can save big and GET ALL 3 BOOKS in one boxed set here.!**

Lastly, **if you enjoyed this book and want to continue to support my writing, please leave this book a review** to let everyone know what you thought of the series. It's the best thing you can do to keep indie authors like me writing. (And if you find something in the book that – YIKES – makes you think it deserves less than 5-stars, drop me a line at Rachel.stoltzfus@globagrafxpress.com, and I'll fix it if I can.)

All the best,

Rachel

ENJOY THIS BOOK? YOU CAN MAKE A BIG DIFFERENCE

Reviews are the most powerful tools in my arsenal when it comes to getting attention for my books. As much as I'd love to, I don't have the financial muscle of a New York publisher. I can't take out full page ads in the newspaper or put up billboards on the highway.

(Not yet, anyway.)

But I have a blessing that is much more powerful and effective than that, and it's something those publishers would do anything to get their hands on.

A loyal and committed group of wonderful readers.

Honest reviews of my books from readers like you help bring them to the attention of other readers.

If you've enjoyed this book, I would be very grateful if you could spend just 3 minutes leaving a review (it can be as short as you like) on this book's review page.

And if, *YIKES* you find an issue in the book that makes you think it deserves less than 5-stars, send me an email at RachelStoltzfus@globalgrafx-press.com and I'll do everything I can to fix it.

Thank you so much!

Blessings,

Rachel S

A WORD FROM RACHEL

Building a relationship with my readers and sharing my love of Amish books is the very best thing about writing. For those who choose to hear from me via email, I send out alerts with details on new releases from myself and occasional alerts from Christian authors like my sister-in-law, Ruth Price, who also writes Amish fiction.

And if you sign up for my reader club, you'll get to read all of these books on me:

1. A digital copy of **Amish Country Tours**, retailing at $2.99. This is the first of the Amish Country Tours series. About the book, one reader, Angel exclaims: " Loved it, loved it, loved it!!! Another sweet story from Rachel Stoltzfus."

2. A digital copy of **Winter Storms**, retailing at $2.99. This is the first of the Winter of Faith series. About the book, Deborah Spencer raves: " I LOVED this book! Though there were central characters (and a love story), the book focuses more on the community and how it comes together to deal with the difficulties of a truly horrible winter."

3. A digital copy of **Amish Cinderella 1-2**. This is the first full book of the Amish Fairy Tales series and retails at 99c. About the book, one reader, Jianna Sandoval, explains: " Knowing well the classic "Cinderella" or rather, "Ashputtle", story by the Grimm brothers, I've do far enjoyed the creativity the author has come up with to match up the original. The details are excruciating and heart wrenching, yet I love this book all the more."

4. A digital copy of **A Lancaster Amish Home for Jacob**, the first of the bestselling Amish Home for Jacob series. This is the story of a city orphan, who after getting into a heap of trouble, is given one last chance to reform his life by living on an Amish farm. Reader Willa Hayes loved the

book, explaining: " The story is an excellent and heartfelt description of a boy who is trying to find his place in the community - either city or country - by surmounting incredible odds."

5. **False Worship 1-2**. This is the first complete arc of the False Worship series, retailing at 99c. Reader Willa Haynes recommends the book highly, explaining: " I gave this book a five star rating. It was very well written and an interesting story. Father and daughter both find happiness in their own way. I highly recommend this book."

You can get all five of these books **for free** by signing up at http://familychristianbookstore.net/Rachel-Starter.

LANCASTER AMISH HOME FOR JACOB SERIES

Orphaned. Facing jail. An Amish home is Jacob's last chance.

The Lancaster Amish Home for Jacob series is the story of how one troubled teen learns to live and love in Amish Country.

BOOK 1: A Home for Jacob

When orphaned Philadelphia teen, Jacob Marshall is given a choice between juvie and life on an Amish farm, will he have the strength to turn his life around? Or will his past mistakes spell an end to his future? Read More.

BOOK 2: A Prayer for Jacob

Just as Jacob's life is beginning to turn around, his long, lost mother shows up and attempts to win him back. Will he chose to stay go with his biological mom back to the Englisch world that treated him so poorly or stay with his new Amish family? Read More.

BOOK 3: A Life for Jacob

When orphaned teen Jacob Marshall makes a terrible mistake, will he survive nature's wrath and truly find his place with the Amish of Lancaster County? Read More.

BOOK 4: A School for Jacob

When Jacob's Amish schoolhouse is threatened by a State teacher who wants to sacrifice their education on the altar of standardized testing, will Jacob and his friends be able to save their school, or will Jacob's attempt to help cost him his new life and home? Read More.

BOOK 5: Jacob's Vacation

When Philadelphia teen, Jacob Marshall goes on vacation to Florida with his Amish family, things soon get out of hand. Will he survive a perilous boat trip, and Sarah the perils of young love? Read More.

BOOK 6: A Love Story for Jacob

When love gets complicated for Jacob, what will it mean for his future and that of his new Amish family? Read More.

BOOK 7: A Memory for Jacob

When anger leads to a terrible accident, will orphaned Philadelphia teen, Jacob Marshall, regain the memories of his Amish life before it's too late? Read More.

BOOK 8: A Miracle for Jacob

When Jacob Marshall makes a promise far too big for him, it's going to take a miracle for him to keep his word. Will Jacob find the strength to ask for help before it's too late? Or will pride be the cause of his greatest fall? Read More.

BOOK 9: A Treasure for Jacob

When respected community leader, Old Man Dietrich, passes on, Jacob discovers that the old man has hidden a treasure worth thousands on his land. Can Jacob and his two best friends solve the mystery and find the treasure before it's too late? Or will this pursuit of wealth put Jacob in peril of losing his new Amish home? Read More.

Or save yourself a few bucks & GET ALL 9-BOOKS in the Boxed Set.

FRIENDSHIP. BETRAYAL. LOVE

SIMPLE AMISH LOVE SERIES

The Simple Amish Love 3-Book Collection is a series of Amish love stories that shows how the power of love can overcome obsession and betrayal. Join the ladies of Peace Landing as they hold onto love in Lancaster County!

BOOK 1 – Simple Amish Love

She's found love. But will a stalker end it all?

After traveling for rumspringa, Annie Fisher returns to her Amish community of Peace Landing ready to take her Kneeling Vows and find a husband. And when handsome Mark Stoltzfus wants to court with her, it seems like everything is going to plan. But when a stalker tries to ruin Annie's relationship, will she be strong enough to stand up for herself?

And will her fragile new romance survive? Read More!

BOOK 2 – Simple Amish Pleasures

A new school year. A new teacher. A hidden danger.

Newly minted Amish teacher, Annie Fisher is ready to start a new school year in Peace Landing. Having been baptized over the summer, Annie is excited to begin her life as an Amish woman. And when the Wedding season arrives, she and Mark will be married. But there is a hidden danger that threatens everything Annie wants, everything she's worked for, and everything she loves. Can Annie face it, and if she does, will it destroy her? Read More.

BOOK 3 – Simple Amish Harmony

She's in love. With the brother of the woman who betrayed her best friend.

Jenny King is elated with her new love, Jacob Lapp. But a cloud hangs over their developing relationship. Jacob's sister betrayed Jenny's best friend, Annie Fisher and has now been cast out of the church. What happens next could spell the end of Jenny's future plans, and the simple harmony of her dreams. Read More.

Or SAVE yourself a few bucks & GET ALL 3-BOOKS the Boxed Set.

A WIDOW. A NEW BUSINESS.
LOVE?

AMISH COUNTRY TOURS SERIES

Join Amish widow, Sarah Hershberger as she opens her home for a new business, her heart to a new love, and risks everything for a new future.

Book 1: Amish Country Tours

When Amish widow, Sarah Hershberger, takes the desperate step to save herself and her family from financial ruin by opening her home to Englisch tourists, will her simple decision threaten the very foundation of the community she loves? Read More.

Book 2: Amish Country Tours 2

Just as widow, Sarah Hershberger's tour business and her courtship with neighbor and widower, John Lapp, is beginning to blossom, will a bitter community elder's desire to 'put Sarah in her place' force her and her family to lose their place in the community forever? Read More.

Book 3: Amish Country Tours 3

Can widow Sarah Hershberger and her new love John Lapp stand strong in the face of lies, spies, and a final, shocking betrayal? Read More.

Or SAVE yourself a few bucks & GET ALL 3-BOOKS in the Boxed Set.

FRIENDSHIP. DANGER. COURAGE

AMISH COUNTRY QUARREL SERIES

Join best friends Mary and Rachel as they navigate danger, temptation, and the perils of love in the Amish community of Peace Landing in Books 1-4 of the Lancaster Amish Country Quarrel series. Read More!

BOOK 1 - An Amish Country Quarrel

When Mary Schrock tries to convince her best friend Rachel Troyer to leave their Amish community and move to the big city, will a simple quarrel spell the end of their friendship? Read More!

BOOK 2 – Simple Truths

When best friends, Mary Shrock and Rachel Troyer, are interviewed by an Englisch couple about their Amish lifestyle, will the simple truth put both girls, and their Amish community, in mortal peril? Read More!

BOOK 3 – Neighboring Faiths

Is love enough for Melinda Abbott to turn her back on her Englisch life and career? And if so, will the Amish community she attempted to harm ever accept her? Read More!

BOOK 4 – Courageous Faith

Before Melinda Abbott can truly embrace her future with her Amish beau, Steven Mast, will she have the courage to face the cult she broke free of in order to pull her cousin from their grasp? Read More!

Or SAVE yourself a few bucks & GET ALL 4-BOOKS in the Boxed Set.

HARDSHIP. CLASH OF WORLDS.
LOVE

WINTER OF FAITH

Join Miriam Bieler and her Amish community as they survive hardship, face encroachment from the outside world, and find love!

BOOK 1: Winter Storms

When a difficult winter leads to tragedy, will the faith of this Ephrata Amish community survive a series of storms that threaten their resolve to the core? Read More.

Book 2: Test of Faith

When Miriam Beiler, a first class quilter, narrowly avoids an accident with an Englischer who asks her for directions to a nearby high school, will this chance meeting push Miriam and her Amish community to an ultimate test of faith? Read More.

Book 3: The Wedding Season

When another suitor wants to steal John away from Miriam, who will see marriage in the upcoming wedding season? Read More.

Or SAVE yourself a few bucks & GET ALL 3-BOOKS in the Boxed Set.

A DANGEROUS LOVE. SECRETS.
TRIUMPH

FALSE WORSHIP SERIES

When Beth Zook's daed starts courting a widow with a mysterious past, will Beth uncover this new family's secrets before she loses everything?

SAVE yourself a few bucks & GET ALL 4-BOOKS in the Boxed Set.

CINDERELLA. SLEEPING
BEAUTY. SNOW WHITE

AMISH FAIRY TALES SERIES

Set in a whimsical Lancaster County of fantastic
possibility grounded in strong Christian values, join
sisters Ella, Zelda and Gerta as they struggle to find
themselves and their places in a world fraught with
peril where nothing is as it seems.

**SAVE yourself a few bucks & GET ALL 4-
BOOKS in the Boxed Set.**

OTHER TITLES

A Lancaster Amish Summer to Remember

When troubled teen, Luke King, is sent for the
summer to live with his uncle Hezekiah on an Amish
farm, will he be able to turn his life around? And

what about his growing interest in their neighbor, 16-year-old Amish neighbor Hannah Yoder, whose dreams of an English life may end up risking both of their futures? Read More.

ACKNOWLEDGMENTS

I have to thank God first and foremost for the gift of my life and the life of my family. I also have to thank my family for putting up with my crazy hours and how stressed out I can get as I approach a deadline. In addition, I must thank the ladies at Global Grafx Press for working with me to help make my books the best they can be. And last, I thank you, for taking the time to read this book. God Bless!

And if you want to keep up with new releases from me, just pop over and join my reader list here :)

ABOUT THE AUTHOR

Rachel was born and raised in Lancaster, Pennsylvania. Being a neighbor of the Mennonite community, she started writing Amish romance fiction as a way of looking at the Amish community. She wanted to present a fair and honest representation of a love that is both romantic and sweet. She hopes her readers enjoy her efforts.

You can keep up with her new releases, discounts and specials when you sign up for **Rachel's email updates list**.

Made in the USA
Monee, IL
28 June 2025

20195588R00098